PUT YOUR LIFE IN THE POT

JAMES MAXWELL

PUT YOUR LIFE IN THE POT

First Edition, 2025

Cover Design by Craig Terlson

Interior Design by Jourdan Dunn

ISBN: 979-8-9913094-3-1 (pbk)
ISBN: 979-8-9913094-2-4 (ebook)

Dedicated to Colin Bailey,
the new man on the block

Part One — Small Blind

1

I NEVER REALLY GOT MY CHANCE, did I? It fucked me up thinking about it. I came from an upper-middle class white suburban family, and what'd I have to show for it? A shitty job any dipshit could hold and an overpriced apartment in a town full of overpaid tech workers and trust fund dickheads. I even had to live with roommates, for Christ's sake.

We were closing up Calvin's Liquors that night. I counted out the register while my coworker, roommate, and so-called friend — the stone-cold fuckin' psychopath that he was — mopped the floor and loudly complained about the state of things.

"I'm tellin' ya," said Joey Patrone. "It's bullshit. He runs off to Key West or wherever, and we're stuck dealing with the alkies and tramps and such. It's a shit deal is what it is."

Joey was a certified douchebag. Everybody knew that, but he didn't have a sense of humor about himself, so no one ever said anything to his face unless they were looking for a fight. I was just about the only guy in San Jose who still hung out with him. But we lived and worked together, so it wasn't like I had a choice. I nodded and stacked the money in the safe.

The liquor store reeked of disinfectant. I shut the safe, spun the dial, and then walked past Joey and his mop to grab a six-pack of IPAs from the beer fridge. I wheeled to face him, shoes squeaking on the floor, and said, "Let's have a few on him then."

We closed shop and headed home to the apartment we shared with a Denny's waitress, Marianne. She hardly spent any time there except refueling for work. I figured she stayed at a boyfriend's place most nights, so this was effectively a two-man spot. Pretty cool deal, if you asked me. We took our spots on the couch, turned on the TV, and cracked our first beers of the night.

"This is some real bullshit," Joey reiterated.

I sipped my beer and thought carefully about my next words. "You wanna do something about it?"

He cocked an eye at me. "Jesus, man. You're not *scheming* now, are you?"

"Shit, yeah, I got a real good plan. So first, we gotta get real drunk. I mean, total blackout, ya know?"

"I like this plan so far."

"Then we'll roll downtown and pick up a couple of those girls you know. Do a little coke, fuck their brains out. And we'll drop them off, blow down 17 in your car with the top off, wash out the sweat with a little wind bath."

Joey nodded with a fat grin.

"Then we'll swing into the barrier." I smacked one palm into the other. "Bam. Out like a light. Never know what hit us."

Joey cackled and downed his beer. "You got a weird-ass sense of humor."

"I'm not joking," I said. "I'm down if you're down."

"I'm down for the part where we get hookers and blow," Joey said with a chuckle. "Not so much the ritual suicide."

I burst out laughing and swigged back my beer. "Fine, seriously then. Wanna get laid tonight?"

"Hell yeah."

...

MY PARENTS BOTH DIED when I was young – my mother at 17 and my father at 18. She died of cancer, then he offed himself six months later. I dodged the foster system a few weeks shy of my birthday. That could've been a good thing, but it earned me a comically harsh introduction to adulthood. The house fell into my name along with almost a hundred-thousand dollars of debt.

Anyway, once I sold the house and paid everything off, I ended up with a surplus of $10k. I spent four grand renting my first apartment, and the other six kept me afloat for a few months while I looked for a decent paying tech job like my dad.

Obviously that was a bunch of bullshit, and it didn't work out. Once I emptied my savings, I started working fast food jobs just to pay the bills while I looked for my real career. That was six years ago.

Four years after that, I reconnected with Joey for the first time since we graduated, and we got an apartment and a job working together at Calvin's. After that I dropped all pretense of looking for a lucrative career in tech.

Mom and dad must be rolling in their fuckin' graves.

Calvin Lenard came home from Key West a few days later, all cheery moods and good spirits with stories about chasing exotic animals and guzzling booze in paradise. One night, somebody had brought a pet monkey into the bar, and it was all fun and games until it started shitting all over the place. We had a good laugh over that one. Around noon, he was back to being his same old miserable pile of assholes.

"I saw the recording," he said. "He held up the beers and said something to you. Then you guys walked out without paying for it."

He had hands on his hips like an angry schoolteacher. I kicked back in the plastic folding chair with my feet crossed under the counter and a business 101 book propped in my lap. For now, I'd set it aside so I could enjoy the daily bitchfest. Joey was leaning on the counter next to the register, and he threw up his hands with a comically exaggerated expression of incredulous disbelief.

"We were gonna tell you when you got back."

"Oh, really? When?"

"I'm tellin' you now, for Christ's sake," he whined. "Just take it out of my paycheck if it's such a big fuckin' deal."

"Next time either of you steal from me," Calvin said, "I'm not just gonna fire you. I'm gonna press charges."

"Go ahead," Joey growled. "See how that works out."

Calvin stormed through a door marked **PRIVATE** and slammed it shut behind him. The noise reverberated in the empty liquor store.

"Jesus," I said. "And I thought the time off might chill him out."

"Are you shitting me? I bet all that sun and hot ass just pissed him off even more, the fuckin' bastard."

It was ten 'til eleven in the morning, and the degenerate alkies were lined up out front, all according to schedule. I picked up my book and kept reading. Joey stuck his hands in his pockets and sauntered over to the front door. Through the glass, the alkies saw him and got excited — *maybe he's opening early today?* Joey reached for the lock, then swung his hand clean past it and slicked back a bit of his hair that'd come undone. He grinned and walked back to the counter.

"One of these days," I said, "they're gonna pull a gun on us. All on account of your dumb ass."

Joey waved me off and said, "Let 'em try it. I'd love to get some target practice."

I laughed nervously. "What do you mean? You're strapped?"

"Hell, yeah. Are you not?"

"Jesus, no," I said. "I don't even have a gun."

Joey raised his shirt. There was a small black Kahr K9 pistol tucked into the waistband of his loose-fitting jeans. The gun looked like it might fall through a leg of his pants with the wrong step.

"Don't you need a holster for that?"

"Hell, nah," Joey said. "That shit's for pussies."

He unlocked the front door at eleven sharp. He would've made those alkies wait another ten minutes just for shits and grins, but Calvin gave him a verbal ass whooping about that last month, and with the bossman already pissed off, I convinced him not to push our luck.

Four people hurried inside the moment Joey unlocked the door. Two of them looked like your typical old-ass bearded degenerates in foul-smelling clothes. Who knew if they were homeless or just looked the part.

The third guy who came in was Andrew Chapman, an old friend I grew up with. We all went to school together: me, him, Joey, and the rest of the guys in the neighborhood. Joey never acted like he knew or even recognized the guy. Maybe they didn't get along, or maybe Joey really didn't remember him. Either way, these days Andrew worked night shift at a local cemetery, so that meant mornings were his evenings.

I perked up and set down my book. The alkies gathered their preferred supply — mainly bottles of hard liquor — and lugged it to the counter for their morning ritual. I rang them up, and meanwhile, Andrew leaned against the counter next to the register. Joey was meandering around the back, loading up stock at a turtle's pace.

"Hey, man," Andrew said. "How's it hanging?"

"Same old shit," I said.

The first alkie paid for a pair of tequila bottles and shuffled away, then came a guy who could barely hold the stack of three twelve-packs he was hoarding for the week. If I knew the guy, I knew he'd back in six days.

"Right on," Andrew said. "So there's gonna be this party down by State tonight. Friend of a friend's spot. You down to hit it up?"

"Ah, I dunno," I said.

"Come on. You could bring Rachel. It'll be fun."

"I don't really talk to her anymore."

"Really? How come?"

"Just cuz."

The next alkie left, and another guy came up to the counter with empty hands. He placed his palms on the counter and stared me down.

"Uh," I said. "Can I help you?"

"I think so, man. You're Tristian Sloan, right?"

"I guess. Who the hell are you?"

"Gilbert," said the guy. "Gil Rodriguez. We graduated Prospect together."

He was a beefy guy with broad shoulders who worked out a lot, but he was short as shit, big and small at the same time. He had one of those smiles that made me want to wince. I remembered after I thought about it a second. He just didn't stand out much from the rest of the assholes I went to school with.

"Oh, yeah." I smirked. "You're the guy who smuggled booze into prom and pissed himself."

Gil nodded with a flushed smile and said, "Yeah, man. That was me."

"You remember Andrew?" I gestured at my bud leaning next to the register. "He graduated our class, too."

"Yeah, sure. What's up, man?"

Andrew nodded and said nothing.

"So, uh," I said. "What's up?"

"Lemme get a couple of those gold Swishers. And a lighter too."

"You got it."

Andrew smirked and said, "Blazin' up, huh?"

"Hell, yeah."

I rang him up, and he said, "Thanks, man. Take it easy."

After he left, Joey came out of the storage room and said, "Who the hell was that?"

"That was Gil," I said. "The fuckin' goober who pissed himself at prom. You don't remember him?"

"Why would I remember a guy like that?"

"He was all right," Andrew chimed in.

Joey shot a glare at him and said, "Are you gonna buy something or what?"

Andrew faced up and said, "Do we got a problem?"

"Relax," I said and got between them. "Andrew's cool. I told him he can hang here."

"Whatever," Joey said. "I'm gonna have a smoke. Cover for me, will ya?"

Without waiting for an answer, he whipped a cigarette out of its pack and strolled out the back. Andrew watched him go, careful to wait until the door was shut before he said anything.

"What the fuck's his deal?" he said.

"He's a bit high-strung. I think he's just unhappy."

"About what?"

"Ah, I dunno," I said. "This and that. All kinds of shit. Just life in general, ya know?"

Andrew nodded and didn't say anything.

"Anyway," I said, "what time's that party tonight? I'll maybe hit her up."

2

JOEY AND I GOT OFF late that night. We were smoking and drinking at our apartment just south of midnight. He was distracted on his phone, probably texting one of those downtown whores. It got me thinking about that party again, thinking about pussy, and thinking about Rachel Mullens.

She was my old flame, and I hadn't talked to her in months. Now seemed like a good time to text her. I asked if she wanted to hit a party tonight. She replied ten minutes later with a quick, *What time?*

And just like that, I had a date. I put on my clean black slacks and a dark pinstriped button-down shirt that I'd only worn once or twice since its last run in the wash. The shirt was a bit ruffled, but it smelled fine, so I buttoned it up. A couple sprays of cologne would cover up any rank leftover from my last escapade.

I drove downtown with the windows rolled down. My car wasn't a convertible like Joey's, and it wasn't nearly as fast or as cool-looking, but it'd been washed and waxed, and it got me from point A to point B. That was all I really cared about. I glanced at my reflection in the rear-view and slicked my hair with my fingers. A little heavy with the pomade tonight, but whatever.

Parking was a pain in the ass. That was par for the course in downtown San Jose, even in a residential neighborhood. I locked my car a few blocks away, lit up a cigarette, and walked down the street. Judging by all the noise and rowdy kids down the road, this seemed like the right spot.

A couple guys were play-fighting in the street, wrestling and jabbing each other like a pair of queers. Might as well fuck and get it over with. I went past them and walked up the lawn to the front door of a townhouse with a shabby coat of pale-purple paint. To my surprise, the door was locked. I knocked and rang the doorbell.

The guy who answered looked none too friendly, some bearded old bastard with a scar on his lip and a cataract in one eye. He glared at me and said, "What?"

"Andrew invited me," I said. "Andrew Chapman. Do you know him?"

The man sneered. For a second there, I wasn't sure if he was gonna shake my hand or punch me in the mouth. He swung the door open and gestured for me to come inside. I hesitated wondering, *Is this even the right house?* while a cacophony of noise raged inside like the crowd at a ballgame. A bunch of people were milling around inside with red Solo cups. It looked like any other party.

"You comin' in or not?" snarled the man.

The atmosphere wasn't quite what I had expected. It was less of a house party and more a noise concert. Some pulsating drone came humming in from the back room where a bunch of people crowded around a guy and his keyboard. Apparently this shit passed for music if you were drunk or stupid enough. I threaded through the crowd and found the beer coolers. They were empty except a sad selection of nonalcoholic beers in half-melted ice. I cussed under my breath and thought it was time to head home.

Someone tapped my shoulder. Some blond beefcake with huge muscles stood next to the cooler with his short shorts and no shirt. He looked like he was standing guard for the pillow-biter battalion.

"There's a keg in the kitchen," he grunted.

"Thanks," I said.

The kitchen was lit up by a cheap Halloween store disco ball. The flashing lights hurt my eyes. I squeezed past a couple making out against the fridge, grinding to the senseless rhythm of the noise emanating from the next room. They might as well have been fucking right there. I choked down a gag and skirted through the kitchen until I found the storied keg.

It was empty too.

"Son of a bitch."

I checked my phone. A text from Rachel said, *Where are you?*

The kitchen, I typed back.

Me too, the reply came right away.

Like a scene in a movie, I looked up and there she was. Rachel wore her loose button-up shirt over a tank top and those skinny black jeans she knew I liked. She smiled with those glossy kiss-me lips and waited for me to approach her.

I went over to her and said, "There's no fuckin' booze." In retrospect, it wasn't the sexiest opener.

"We've got some more out back," she said.

I followed her through the garage, where a bunch of kids were smoking weed from a gravity bong. They'd constructed the contraption out of a big plastic cubby and some cut-up plastic milk jug. Each hit off that thing must've been like smoking ten joints at once. A girl was on her back, coughing her lungs out while the chief of the circle packed the next bowl.

We stepped into the backyard, where the talk and laughter echoed in the night. It'd be a miracle if no neighbors called the cops. But for now, we enjoyed the party while it lasted.

Rachel led me back to the corner, where they'd set up a beer pong table. About a dozen guys were playing, and they all looked like palette swaps of some cartoon frat boy. Behind the ping-pong table, in the corner of the yard where the grass was overgrown, there were three lawn chairs half-circling someone's backpack like it was a campfire.

Someone was in the middle chair, a big guy kicked back in cargo shorts with his hairy legs exposed and his sleeping face hidden under a hat. Rachel brought me over and gestured to the backpack.

"We've got Sierras in the bag," she said.

"Don't mind if I do," I said. I riffled through and grabbed a can. No bottles? Damn, what a bummer. Rachel took an empty chair, and I sat opposite her.

"Oh, hold up," she said. "I think someone's sitting there."

"They're not anymore."

Rachel chuckled and said, "I guess not."

The man in the middle chair was fast asleep. He could've been dead for all I knew. Someone got pissed at the beer pong table, and a couple frat boys started yelling at each other. A third guy settled their beef by telling them both to chill out and have a drink.

It might've been the beer, but Rachel looked a lot hotter than I remembered. Her dark hair was partially braided into a heap with artfully mussed bangs hanging over her brows. She had the messy hairstyle thing down to a science. I couldn't help but admire her, and she caught my staring eyes.

She smiled and waited for me to say something, but nothing came to mind. "So how's work been?" she said.

I didn't reply. I just chuckled and sipped my drink.

"I was wondering when you were gonna hit me up," she said.

"I didn't think you wanted to see me."

"I'm sorry I got pissed. I was just in a bad mood is all."

"It's all right," I said. "I was forty minutes late."

She chuckled and said, "Did you ever do that thing you were talking about doing?"

I knew exactly what she was talking about. "What are you talking about?"

"You know," she said. "Your boss was always such an asshole. You always said, nobody would care if somebody—"

"I saw your sister the other day, actually," I interrupted. "She came in and bought three bottles of Jack."

She pursed her lips and nodded. "Sounds like Janene to me."

"You seen Andrew around here? I thought he'd be here."

"No," she said.

We sat for a while and sipped our drinks while we watched the beer pong game play out. It was getting down to the wire. Three cups left versus one, but the one team was up. If they made no more mistakes, they could win the game.

The next man up made a mistake. He was that blond beefcake I ran into inside, and he was already too drunk off his ass to have any sort of hand-eye coordination. He tossed the ball, and it bounced off one cup rim, then the other, before it sailed off the table.

"Oof," Rachel said. "That's the game right there."

She gave me a look that I tried not to notice, like the way your mother might look at you when she's worried you're hurt.

"Hey," she said.

I snapped my attention at her. We locked eyes, and I remembered how beautiful they were. Green or brown or hazel or whatever the fuck. I didn't know, and it didn't really matter.

"Are you okay?" she said.

Something overwhelmed me that I didn't like to acknowledge. A wave of hurt and regret. We never dated all that long, if we even dated at all. And it was never that serious. But it felt so wrong sitting here talking to her. All I could think about was the other night with Joey and the get-rich-quick plan he told me about after we fucked the brains out of those two whores. Now her eyes were hard to look at.

"Yeah," I said. I finished my beer and crushed the can between my palms. "Got any more?"

"Those were the last two," she said.

"That's all right." I stood up from the chair and stretched. "I should probably go."

"Really?" she said. "We just got here."

"I gotta get up early for work."

I left the party and walked back to my car through the dark and lonely night. A certain numbness drove down to my core, like a fire snuffed out in the cold. I stuck my hands in my pockets and rubbed my palms against my thighs. There were stars bright in the night sky. I didn't pay much attention to them these days, but when I looked up, I could've sworn I saw that Big Dipper thing my mom used to talk about. Or was it the Little Dipper? I wished I could ask her. I missed her so.

A coldness lingered in my heart. I didn't quite know what it was or why it was there. But it drove me to do what I knew I shouldn't. I was going to make out of this with a lot of money. One way or another. I didn't care where it came from.

THE NEXT DAY, I woke up with the mother of all headaches, and I popped an Ibuprofen and smoked a bowl before I went into work. Joey wasn't scheduled for today. Lucky bastard was still asleep in his room.

If there was one thing I couldn't complain about, it was the commute. I hopped into my car and in three minutes flat I was parking in the Calvin's Liquors lot. I locked my car next to a purple BMW that I swear I'd seen before. It was never a good sign to see this particular kind of car at a place like this.

The front door was unlocked. I swung it open and stepped inside, and the lights were off. Some commotion came from the back office.

I opened the back door marked **PRIVATE**. There was a massive doughball of a man inside pinning Calvin to his desk. A woman stood back with her arms crossed and observed them both. She wore black slacks and a loose white button-down shirt with a puffy peacoat. She shot her eyes at me when I entered the room.

"Who the fuck are you?" she said.

"Tristian," I stammered. "I work here."

They were both Vietnamese. And since they were kicking the shit out of Calvin, that could only mean one thing. They were part of that gang who owned the shop, and they were the ones Calvin paid off every week.

The woman snapped her fingers, and the guy let Calvin go. He fell coughing and wheezing to the floor. The man and woman streamed out of the office and gave me a hard stare on their way out. I waited until they left before I said anything.

"What the fuck?" I said. "I thought this was your place. Your name's on the sign."

"Yeah, well. Not anymore." He stood up, coughing, and picked up his chair from where it'd been knocked over. "Go grab us a drink, will ya?"

I grabbed a six-pack from the fridge and set it down on the counter, then I cracked two bottles and laid them out on the counter. We took a nice big morning swig together.

"So what's goin' on then, Cal?" I said. "I mean, I knew those guys owned the place, but shit. Isn't that enough? Why do they gotta come in here and slap you around like that?"

He explained the situation in short terms: It was a gambling thing. Calvin had gambled away the store, and then he kept gambling. Maybe some part of him held out hope he'd win big one day, be able to buy the place back. But that was the long and short of it.

"Jesus," I said. "You ever considered gamblers anonymous?"

"Don't lecture me, Tris," Calvin said. "I get enough shit from my wife."

"Relax. I'm just breaking your balls. I know how you feel, man."

I raised my bottle for a cheers. Calvin hesitated and obliged.

"What time is it?" he said.

"Ten 'til. I'll go open up shop. You just sit back and relax, okay?"

The alkies made their usual rounds. A few graybeards who smelled like shit, plus my good ol' buddy Andrew. Once the degenerates were gone, Andrew grabbed his usual pair of tall boys and set them on the counter. I rang him up and he paid, then he cracked a can and started drinking on the spot. He leaned against the counter and burped.

"Hey, man," I said. "Where were you last night? I didn't see you at the party."

He shrugged. "I was dancing in the garage. Guess we just missed each other."

"For sure, man. Hey, So I was just wondering. You make good money at your job?"

Andrew cocked an eye at me. "Sure, I dunno." He sipped his tall boy.

"I mean, good enough you could just quit for a while?"

"Fuck no. But who does, right?"

"So there's this thing going on with Joey. It's kind of a rip-and-dip maneuver, you know?"

Andrew swirled the tall boy in his hand. He was completely clueless.

The door marked **PRIVATE** clicked and swung open. Calvin stomped out and pointed at Andrew. "That's an open container. Get it out."

"Sorry, man." He took his beers and was ready to shuffle before I grabbed his arm and whispered to him.

"I'm off at three. I'll come to your place."

"My place?"

"Mine's not safe to chat."

When I left work, I headed over to Andrew's house instead of driving home. It was a nice little property in the suburbs of West San Jose. They lived a couple blocks away from the light rail and a strip mall with some decent food joints. I parked right down the street, no more than a dozen yards away. What a thing that was, just to park and walk in. At my apartment, I had to fight tooth and nail for a decent spot or else walk three or more blocks from my car.

He had inherited this place from his parents when they died about a decade back. Lucky for him, they weren't loaded with debt, so he actually got to live in the house. His wife worked a part-time day job to help them get by. I guess late-night cemetery watchmen didn't get a very generous pay.

I rang the doorbell, and Andrew opened the door and showed me his idyllic American life: his hot wife, a homemaker, cool but not too ambitious or annoying, and a young son in his image. A legacy or a lineage or whatever the fuck. It pissed me off thinking about it. It's not that I wanted any of that. I just wanted the privilege of saying no.

We made small talk for all of five seconds before I couldn't help it anymore. "I need to talk to you, man."

"Relax," he whispered. "Don't wanna spook my wife."

It took ten minutes to extricate ourselves from that mess. We went into the garage on the pretense of firing off some airsoft pellets at the target on the wall. Andrew warned his wife not to open the door without knocking first lest a stray pellet hit her.

There was no car in the garage, just a bunch of heavyweight badass type shit like the airsoft target and a boxing bag and some dumbbells. Andrew walked over to the table and picked up a plastic M9. He turned to face me, and a wave of panic washed over me like I even had a gun on my hip to reach for if something went bad.

"Sorry." Andrew chuckled. He clearly saw that. "I didn't mean to startle you. It's just an airsoft."

He pointed the pistol at the garage door and squeezed the trigger, popping off a plastic pellet that punched right through the paper target and caught in the felt net behind it.

"I know."

"What'd you wanna talk about?" he said.

I let out a heavy sigh. Right now I wished I had a drink in my hands. I thought about asking for one, but that might add unnecessary drama, so I dropped it and drove right to the point.

Andrew didn't really know anything about anything, so I had to explain it pretty thoroughly. Joey and I had a friend who was a professional stickup artist until about two years ago when he tried to rob the Viet mob's VIP game. Naturally, they put him in the ground. Joey brought it up from time to time, always making the point that the guy had made the mistake of going loud when he could've gone quiet.

"Is it starting to make sense?" I said.

Andrew nodded and said, "Yeah, no. Not really."

I told him how my friend Joey from the liquor store was real desperate to get into that VIP game. He had endured some real bullshit to get a crumb of favor from Dennis Phan. And eventually it worked out, because he'd finally been invited to play bagman at the storied VIP game — which meant he'd handle the money after it all wrapped up.

So, naturally, Joey planned to deprive them of their money. It was pretty simple when you broke it down. The VIP game was being hosted at a coffee shop right down the street from Calvin's Liquors. Joey had worked there part-time for the last few months. Officially speaking, he was a backroom stocker, but nobody ever expected him to show up and work in any official capacity. Instead, he'd head there after midnight and spend late mornings playing janitor and bagman for low-stakes games.

But he needed a second man, someone like me, who worked the front of the shop. The recording would show him doing it, but naturally his back would cover the contents of the safe, and he'd sleight-of-hand that shit into his coat pocket. As long as I saw him and backed him up, swore on my life he had really put the money in the safe, he was in the clear. For my trouble, I'd get $2,000.

"So why are you telling me this?" Andrew said.

"Because," I said with a smile. "I'd rather have half."

There was the question of transportation. Joey anticipated that there'd be as much as $2.5 million in a take from the VIP game. Normally such an amount would warrant an armored car, but this was illegal cash we were talking about, and the coffee shop was literally three shops away, so it would've attracted more attention to do anything fancy like that. He'd just walk it down the street.

However, as Joey's brilliant plan went, he'd come back later that night to smash the windows, steal the safe, and erase the security footage. That way it would appear to be a random burglary.

I intended to deprive him of that money before he even arrived at the liquor store. But I needed someone else to do it while I saved face.

Andrew laughed and said, "Seriously?"

I gave him one of those serious looks like I'd never been more serious in my life.

3

OUR LIVING ROOM BILLOWED white wisps of weed smoke. Joey and I were kicking back on the couch watching TV, our feet crossed on the dusty coffee table littered with empty beer bottles and a filthy blackened bong. A woman with blond hair and plastic tits was getting her brains fucked out on TV by some big Black guy.

"Why the fuck are we watching this?" I said.

"What?"

I took my feet off the table and flicked through the channels with the remote control.

"Hey, man," Joey said. "I paid two dollars for that."

"I'll buy you a beer. Make up the difference." I landed on a channel playing a censored version of *Goodfellas*. Joe Pesci just called some wiseguy a "muddaflippa," only it wasn't Pesci's voice saying the line, but some poorly paid voice actor who vaguely sounded like him.

"Fuck this movie, man," Joey moaned. "It's a bunch of bullshit."

"What do you mean?"

"These guys don't know shit about being gangster. Just look at De

Niro. He was born in New York, sure, but he went to a conservatory. He's a fuckin' theater kid, for Chrissake."

"Well, yeah," I said. "They're actors. What'd you expect? They're going around Harlem looking for badass motherfuckers to play these roles?"

"He thinks he's so goddamn tough." Joey sipped his beer, and he took his feet off the table and started packing a bowl in the bong. "I bet I'm tougher than him."

"Well, sure, man," I said. "It's just make-believe. What, you think they really shot Joe Pesci in the head or something?"

"No, obviously they're not gonna kill him for the movie. Are you shitting me? There's money to be made with more movies, sequels and franchise bullshit like that." He sparked the lighter and sucked the bowl through the bong. The filthy water bubbled, and the smoke was sucked through the tube. Then he leaned back and coughed up a lungful.

I genuinely couldn't find any words, so I did what I do best and didn't say shit. I just changed the channel and looked for something else to watch.

"Well, hey, I didn't tell you to turn it off," Joey said between coughs. "I was just saying it sucks."

"So whatever happened to our VIP game?"

"What do you mean? Nothing happened, it's still on." Joey set the bong down and kicked his legs up on the table.

"I mean, we never ironed out when it's going down."

"Next Sunday," he stated plainly. The easy answer took me off-guard.

"Oh yeah?"

"Yeah." He gave me a hard look as if he was sizing me up. That didn't make a lot of sense considering we'd lived together for years now. What could he possibly see now that he didn't already know about me?

"Slight change of plans," he said. "So this VIP game, right? They start on Friday and wrap up around 9:00 p.m. on Sunday. Real heavyweights, they go at it nonstop. Anyway, they asked me to hang around, so I figure I'll be the bagman that night. Once it's all wrapped, I'll bring the package back to Calvin's – where you'll be working."

"Yeah, like most nights."

"I'll show up and stick the money in the safe like normal. Then we'll lock it up, I'll head home, and you continue with your shift like nothing happened.

"Now this is the fun part." Joey grinned. "You'll close up at eleven like usual, then head home. I'll wait outside for Calvin to leave after you, then I'll break into the place, take the money, and turn off the cameras and delete the footage."

"But they're gonna think he did it," I said.

Joey looked at me blankly and said, "Well, yeah. That's the idea."

"Jesus." I laughed humorlessly. "They're gonna kill him, man."

"So what?"

Goddamn psychopath. That was the substance that made up Joey Patrone. A ruthless fucking bastard who'd put anyone and everyone under the axe if it meant a big payout. I couldn't help myself from wondering if Joey had some plans worked out for me that I wasn't privy to.

"Okay." I nodded slowly, thinking this whole thing through. "So Calvin dies. Then what?"

"Then you get your cut." He said it so matter-of-factly, like it was a foregone conclusion. "If you got a problem with that, you can always back out."

"I'm not backing out," I said. "It's just—wow. We're really gonna do Calvin like that?"

"Yeah, fuck him. Hope he enjoyed Key West, the son of a bitch."

We cracked some beers and smoked more bowls and watched a game show on television. Steve Harvey had a hyperbolic expression of shock, confusion, and disbelief after a contestant's zany answer. Some hilarious stuff if you had brain damage.

There was one thing I learned that night, which proved to be both invaluable information and the key to all my fuckups. I realized right there that I shouldn't feel the least bit sorry for fucking over Joey and costing him his life. He would do me the same in a heartbeat.

Part Two — Big Blind

4

AFTER WORK THE NEXT DAY, I headed to that videogame-themed
bar in downtown San Jose that my friends were all hyped up about
some years back. It looked sad and dead tonight. The arcade cabinets
glowed enticing start screens to no audience. Nobody was playing
pool, air hockey, or any of the other usual crowd draws. A few perpet-
ual alcoholics hovered around the bar counter.

I spotted Andrew right away. He was the only guy here to play
games, hovering over the Mortal Kombat III booth with his head
hunched down and his eyes locked on the screen. He twisted the joystick around and smashed the buttons. I ordered a pair of drinks and
went over. Andrew was playing Sub Zero in single-player. He shot an
ice bolt at Liu Kang, froze him, and shattered his body in an impres-
sive feat of violence.

"Hey, man," I said. "You training for a tourney or something?"

"Nah." Andrew wiped the sweat from his brow. "This is just my
spot when I wanna duck my wife."

"You must be the only guy here actually gaming."

"I mean, yeah. It's a Tuesday night. What do you expect?"

I hadn't really paid attention to the day of the week these last few nights. Like I was floating in space. All I could think about was a big payout coming my way, or else a slow and painful death.

"So what's up, man?" Andrew said. He took his beer and leaned against the game booth. "Come here to watch me fiddle with my joystick?"

"I got news from Joey. We're on for Sunday."

Andrew got quiet all of a sudden. He pursed his lips, nodded, and didn't say anything.

"Is something wrong?"

"It's just, I dunno." He took a swig of his beer. "This whole thing's starting to feel risky."

"Of course it's risky. Or else it wouldn't be worth it."

"I know, I know." Andrew sighed. "But Jesus, man. These are serious guys we're dealing with. If we fuck this up, you know what they'll do?"

"Sure, I know what they'll do."

"They'll kill our families and fuckin' torture us to death."

"You've seen too many movies." I sipped my beer. "Anyway, we got a cover and a fall guy. So we're good to go."

Andrew squinted and said, "What the hell are you talking about?"

I took a deep breath and carefully considered my next words. "I like to think that you and me, we're all-right guys. Right?"

He snorted and said, "Yeah, I guess."

"So most of the time, we don't fuck anyone over. We do honest business." I took another swig. "But sometimes there's exceptions. Someone who's just such a piece of shit that they've got it coming. Doesn't matter if they've never wronged you personally."

"Sure, man," Andrew said. "I guess that makes sense."

"The kind of people who wouldn't hesitate to, say, rip someone off and let another man take the fall."

Andrew said, "Wait, are you talking about you or someone else?"

"What?"

"I take it you mean someone else."

The question took me totally off-guard. I stumbled to regain my composure. "Of course I mean someone else. Look, all I'm saying is rules have exceptions. And this is an exception to a pretty serious rule."

"I don't like where you're going with this."

"Let me start over." I drained my beer and set the glass on the table next to the Mortal Kombat booth. "You remember Joey's plan I talked about?"

"Sure."

"Well, we talked things over. The plan just got a little more complicated. He wants Calvin to take the axe."

Andrew cocked an eyebrow and said, "You mean get him killed?"

It was about as plainly as I could've put it. I glanced around to make sure nobody overheard. "Yeah, get him killed. So I propose we make *him* take the fall."

"Who. Calvin?"

"No. Joey, for Christ's sake. Are you listening to me?"

"Oh, right. I just thought cuz Joey's your friend and all."

I opened my mouth to say something but found myself speechless. So I changed the subject. "He said they're gonna be done around 9:00 p.m on Sunday. You hang around the corner and wait for Joey to head out."

"Jesus, man," Andrew said. He sipped his beer and glanced around like he wasn't totally sure of what we were talking about. "I gotta tell you, this doesn't sound all too well thought out."

"I've thought about it. You got a better idea?"

"Yeah. We don't do this. It's fuckin' stupid."

"So you wanna let Calvin die?" I tutted at him. "Come on, man. We're saving his life here. You wanna just step out and do nothing?"

"Don't do that," Andrew said. "Don't go and make this seem noble now."

"If it makes you feel any better."

"Fuck feeling better." Andrew drained his drink. "Come on. Let's go to a real bar."

. . .

RACHEL TEXTED ME a couple nights before the VIP game, when I was nervous as hell and looking for anything to get it off my mind. She asked if I wanted to check out a local band. I asked which band, and she said Necrot. They play death metal. Heavy riffs and blast beats, that kind of thing. I told her sure, I'd be there.

The place was exactly what I had expected: some shitty downtown dive bar that didn't even charge for cover. Rachel wasn't kidding when she said heavy riffs and blast beats. You could feel the notes pummeling your eardrums from down the block. The bar was small and crowded, and it had the look of some kind of rocker bar. The walls were covered in tour posters, framed album art, and various graffiti.

I needled through the crowd and went over to the bar. The stools were all taken, so I had to push my way past a pair of couples who were on some kind of double date given their offended reaction when I pried between them.

"What can I get ya?" said the bartender.

"Lemme get three Sierra Nevadas."

"Small or large?"

"Gimme the big boys."

The song wrapped up, and the crowd started cheering. Some people milled out of the stage room, and others wandered in to take their place. I sipped all three of the beers to mitigate any spillage, then I cupped two under one arm and held the third. I meandered toward the stage, scanning the crowd for any sign of Rachel.

I squeezed into the stage room, which was a little square no larger than the bar itself, maybe a touch smaller. Nothing at all like the concerts I used to attend with my dad before he died. Those were always in big stadiums, the performers like godly monoliths on a massive pedestal before us. Here they just stood in front of the crowd like everybody else. There wasn't really a stage at all. People could just walk up and high-five the band.

"Hey, Tris," her voice came from behind me. I turned to face her and spilled the beers all over my arm. She giggled and kissed my cheek.

Rachel wore a see-through mesh shirt over a tight tank-top shirt. I checked out her body and the way her clothes fit real tight. She had a black miniskirt that showed off the upside-down cross tattoos on the backs of her thighs. A real goth girl, if I'd ever seen one.

"Gimme one of those," she said.

"One of them was for you," I lied. In reality, I was a raging alcoholic at the time. I've cleaned up my act since then, not that it really matters.

"Sure it was." She laughed.

The guitarist fired off a complex sequence of riffs, and the bass man hit some strings to back him up. Then the drummer came in with the crash, and a storm fell over the audience. The vocalist gurgled something that sounded less like song lyrics and more like sound effects from a horror movie.

The bar picked up into a steady onslaught of death metal mayhem, everybody swaying to the rhythm. Some thirty-odd people banged their heads to the crunchy downtuned beat. Rachel bobbed around, spilling the beer in her hand. She was a freak for this weirdo extreme music. I didn't care much for it myself, but I sure liked the way it pumped her up, if only because it guaranteed an easy lay after the show.

A cozy little mosh pit opened up in the room, barely wide enough to contain itself. Everyone who didn't want to get pushed around backed off. I pulled Rachel behind me and formed sort of a wall against the drunken assholes running around. That was our standard procedure, since I knew Rachel wasn't all that into moshing. I finished my beer and tossed the plastic cup in the air, then started working on the next one.

Some short beefy guy pushed through the crowd and made a hard line toward us. Most likely a white knight type who didn't take kindly to crowd unfriendly behavior like cup tossing. I took a big swig and readied myself for a fight.

When the guy approached me, I recognized him right away. But I couldn't quite put the name to his face.

"Hey, Tristian," the man shouted over the noise. "How you doing?"

"What?"

"I said how you doing?"

"Fine," I said, squinting at the guy. I gave up. "Who are you?"

"Gil. I was at your store the other day."

"Oh yeah, that's right. We went to school together."

"We did, yeah."

A big jacked guy with a shiny bald head came flying out of the pit. He was drunk as shit and barely stayed on his feet, slamming right into me and knocking me back a few steps. I shoved the guy back into the pit and reviewed the damage. Half my beer had soaked my pants.

"Jesus," I shouted over the noise. "Fuckin' asshole."

"Lemme buy you another," Gil said. "Come on."

I told Rachel I'd be right back, but she didn't seem to hear me, lost in the rhythm of the music. I followed Gil from the stage room back to the counter. The venue was crowded now and got steadily more packed.

Gil pushed through two guys at the counter and flagged down the bartender. He ordered another pair of big boys and handed one to me. We knocked our plastic cups together.

"Cheers," I said.

"Hell, yeah. So, hey, Tris. I wanted to ask you something."

"What's that?"

"I dunno if you know," Gil said, "but I run with this crew out of the East Side. They're always looking for money to make."

"Isn't everyone?"

Gil grinned and said, "Yeah, sure. But I saw you working the other day, and it got me thinking. What if we set up a kinda business venture?"

"A what?"

The band wrapped up in the other room, and a handful of wild fans yelled their lungs out. Everybody else milled out, and the bar area got even more crowded. That bald sweaty mosher pushed between us to shout an order at the bartender, and the bartender in turn cussed him out. Seemed like a high-strung kind of night.

When the sweaty guy left, Gil did a little *P-U* wave in front of his nose and laughed. He swallowed the last of his beer.

"Calvin's Liquors," he said. "You guys get shipments every week, right?"

"Give or take."

"So I was thinking, maybe my buddy comes by. He picks up a couple cases on the downlow, and you get paid directly." He shrugged. "Or whoever happens to be working that day."

"You want me to steal stock?"

"It's just a little backroom discount." Gil grinned.

"I don't think Calvin's gonna like that."

"Look, if you need help convincing him, I've got a couple buddies who could come—"

"I appreciate the offer," I interrupted. "But I'm gonna have to pass. Calvin lost his shit last week when me and Joey took a six-pack from the fridge. I don't wanna risk it over some bullshit like this."

In truth, me and Joey regularly juiced the place. We had this thing going where we took a salami slice off the top every day. A few bucks out the register here and there adds up over time. Kinda like *Office Space* or *Superman III*. It was bad enough splitting the take with Joey, who probably lied about how much he was taking out the register anyway, but getting a third man involved sounded about as appealing as getting a hole in the back of my head.

Gil pursed his lips and said, "Maybe another time."

Rachel came through the crowd with mascara running in sweaty streaks down her face and an expression that buzzed delight. She practically threw herself on me and pinned me to the counter, then she kissed my cheek and said *hey* to Gil.

"Hiya, Rach," Gil said. "How's the job search going?"

"Pretty rough," she said. "But my parents got me covered. So it's all good."

"What are you talking about?" I said.

"She applied at my dad's company last month. But they didn't hire her."

"For all the good your rec did." She had a pointed smirk on her face.

He put his palms up and said, "Hey, don't look at me. I only work there cuz of my dad. Anyway, I gotta head out. It was good seeing you two."

"You're not gonna stay for Necrot?" Rachel said.

"Nah, I got my hard rock fill for tonight. I gotta get going."

He hugged Rachel and shook my hand, then he shoved through the dense crowd of sweaty metalheads and made his way to the exit.

"Wasn't that who just played?" I said.

"Nah, that was the opener. Necrot's up next. Man, it's so funny seeing Gil here. I didn't think he's a fan of this kinda music."

"He's not."

"What do you mean?"

"Nothing," I said. "How do you know him, anyways?"

"We worked together at Nvidia. Well, we didn't *work* together — he was in HR, but he did my onboarding."

We ordered another round of beers, and Necrot started their sound check in the stage room. The guitarist busted off some crunchy notes and gurgled nonsense words. People started milling toward the stage.

"Let's go," Rachel said.

I didn't have a chance to fight back. She just took me along, and next thing I knew, I was shoulder-to-shoulder with a bunch of moist assholes in all manner of peacockish leather vests and jackets, like this was some kind of fashion show instead of a concert. I slurped down half my beer to cool myself off in the humid room, and Rachel hung on to my arm. For a minute there, I thought she was just too drunk to stand up. But when the lights dimmed and she started hollering and clapping, it dawned on me that she might actually like me.

The band was just a bunch of regular guys. Their hair was a bit long, sure. Their clothes were dirty and ripped up, and you could smell them before they took the stage. But they weren't done up in black-and-white makeup or anything like I expected from a death metal show. There was no animal blood or ritual sacrifice. Just some dudes banging out riffs. If I'm being honest, I could kinda see the appeal.

The music picked up, and a tight mosh pit formed in the room.

Me and Rachel were right in the middle of it. A bunch of drunk ass-holes thrashed around us, pushing at each other in a clean circle while we stood together in the eye of the storm.

Rachel wrapped her arms and held me tight. Her heart raced against my chest. We hugged in the middle of the pit while the non-sense raged around us. I looked at her and she watched the band, her cheek smooth and delectable in the low light. I leaned in and kissed her neck, and she didn't seem to mind. She threw a hand up and belted out a *Fuck yeah* at the band right before the drummer hit off some nasty blast beats. Things amped up, more people jumped in the pit, and the rhythm of things got all fucked up. Instead of a smooth circle, people shoved in every direction. That same bald asshole knocked us over and sprawled us out on the sticky floor.

Feet stormed around us, and the blast beats rained on our ears. I stood up and dragged Rachel with me. We were on our feet by the time a bystander offered a hand to help us. I thanked the man, and we pushed dazedly back through the crowd until we were out the door and back in the barroom again, where the cool air from outside washed us over and felt like a shower from the heavens.

"Damn," she said. "That hurt."

"I thought it was kinda fun."

We looked at each other again, and we didn't look away. Something painful warmed up in my soul, like an engine of forethought and regret.

I kissed Rachel, and right then I knew I would soon die.

When we pulled away, she giggled at me with a smug look of sur-prise.

"Where'd that come from?" she said.

"I don't know," I said. "I'm sorry."

"Are you kidding?" She laughed and kissed me again. "Come on. Let's go back in."

"I don't feel good."

I rushed away and stumbled into the bathroom. There was a line for the toilets, but I couldn't hold it back. I bent over a trashcan and puked into a pile of wet paper towels. The sweaty guys in line laughed, and I staggered over to the sink and washed my mouth out. Rachel was waiting for me back in the barroom.

"You all good?" she said.

"Yeah. I'm good. Just maybe don't kiss me for a while."

We went into the stage room and hovered in the back with the other low-energy meanderers. There was a hot young couple leaned against the wall, too busy making out to notice that a band was playing music. We stood next to them, Rachel bobbing her head to the beat while I held my arm around her neck and sipped my beer.

After the show, we wandered through the cool summer air of the downtown streets. A bunch of sweaty concertgoers meandered around and filed away from the venue. Me and Rachel held each other tight while we walked back to her car.

I pressed her against the driver door and put my hands on her hips, hers around my back, and we made out. Then she pulled back and said, "Wanna go back to my place?"

"I don't think that's a good idea." I regretted saying it as soon as I saw the look on her face.

"What do you mean?"

I wanted to take it back. Make it all okay for us. Say something like I'm just kidding, I'm just shitting you, let's go back to your place and smash as soon as humanly possible.

"I just don't think it's a good idea," I said.

"Why not?"

I kept hearing Andrew's words in my head. *They'll kill our families and fuckin' torture us to death.*

"I just don't wanna get tied down," I said.

She snorted and gave me a look that humiliated me worse than any insult. "If you say so."

I backed off, wiped my lips, and said, "I'm sorry."

"Don't trip about it," she said. "I'll text you, okay?"

Rachel got in the car and fired up the engine. I stood there and watched her pull into the street and cruise away. She got smaller in the distance until I couldn't see her, and it was just me alone on the dark street with my thoughts.

"Goddamnit," I muttered. Then I went back to my car and headed home.

On my way back, I stopped by that place Joey had taken me the other week. I recognized my date from that night. Her name was Lizzy, or that's what she called herself. She smiled when she saw me.

"Hey, baby," she said. "You wanna have some fun?"

"Why do you think I'm here?"

I didn't mean that to sound so angry and sad. She felt it, but she didn't say a word. She just blinked with those big fake eyelashes and an even faker grin. "Okay, honey. Let's go."

I unlocked the door to my apartment and swung it open. Joey was kicking back on the couch watching TV. Our third roommate, Marianne, was grilling sausages in the kitchen.

"Hey, man," Joey said. "You didn't tell me you're getting laid tonight. I'm down."

Marianne kept cooking. She didn't seem to notice or hear anything we were saying. But my face flushed red because I knew she could hear, and she was judging my manhood. I couldn't bring myself to say a word.

"I can call my friend if you want a date, honey," Lizzy said.

"Why don't you do that?" Joey smiled. "Sounds fun."

"Okay, give me a minute." She walked to the bathroom and took her phone out of her purse before she shut herself inside.

Joey stood up and whooped with a clap of the hands. "Fuck yeah."

Our roommate rolled the sausages on the pan and refused even to look back at me or acknowledge my existence. I don't think she'd ever acknowledged my existence since she signed the lease, except maybe saying hi to me once or twice. That really pissed me off, but mostly it made me ashamed and embarrassed.

"I'll be in my room." I shuffled away and shut my bedroom door behind me. Then I looked at my texts with Rachel on my phone. The last thing she said to me was *See you there*. Short and emotionless.

Someone knocked on my door, and I called out to come in. Lizzy opened up and stuck her head in with an uncertain expression, then she came in and shut the door.

I took out my wallet and retrieved three hundred dollars in cash, then I set it atop my dresser. Lizzy counted the money and stuffed it in her purse, and she set it down on the floor along with her coat, her shirt, and her skirt. She was in black lingerie that showed off those perfect plastic tits and ass. She was about to undo her bra before I wrapped my arms around her warm body and did it for her.

"I wanna be the only one," I moaned into her neck.

"Of course you are, sweetie."

She was gone twenty minutes later, and I was three hundred dollars poorer. I sprawled my legs out on my bed, consciously thinking about how laid I just got while I smoked a joint and let the clouds bloom through the bedroom. The last thought running through my mind before I fell asleep had something to do with keeping Rachel safe.

5

I FELT GOOD AS HELL the next morning, and I got out of bed as soon as I woke up. Normally I'd linger and try to squeeze in another forty minutes of sleep, but today seemed like a good day. I took a shower and arrived at the liquor store forty-five minutes before opening. Calvin was out front with a cigarette in the dawn light. The morning round of alkies hadn't even showed up yet.

"How's it goin', Cal?" I said.

He nodded and blew a puff of smoke. "I'm all right. Glad you're here. I wanted to have a chat."

"Ah, shit."

"Nah, don't worry," he said. "It's nothing like that. I just wanted to apologize." He dropped the cigarette on the ground and crushed it under his heel. "The other day, when I blew up, I called you a thief. That's not what you are, even if you do take beers on the house from time to time."

I shrugged and said, "Well, I did. Two of 'em, anyways."

"Whatever, man. My point is that Joey's the real thief. I've seen him taking money out the register. I just wanted you to know, I think you're all right."

It took everything in me to hold back from laughing in his face. I smiled politely and did my best not to look too happy to hear him say this. "No harm, no foul."

"Between you and me, I'm just waiting. Once I get him for over nine-fifty bucks, it'll be a felony. Send his fuckin' ass away."

"Sure, man," I said. "I mean, the guy's a prick. I don't blame ya."

"Come on," Calvin said. He unlocked the door and held it open. "Let's get ready before the morning regulars show up."

We finished opening by 10:50, which was right when the drunks started queuing up for their morning fix. We were both in good moods, so why not give them their daily gratification a little early?

Five minutes before noon, a young woman came into the store wearing a loose crop top over her boyfriend jeans. She had an Indian look to her, stunning as hell if a little overdone on the mascara. I was half asleep at the time, so she probably could've robbed me blind and I never would've been the wiser. But she came up to the counter and knocked my cross-legged feet off the register.

I don't remember what I said, but it must not've been nice, given the look on her face. She chewed me out about shitty customer service and then said, "Is your manager in today?"

"Who's asking?"

The **PRIVATE** door clicked and swung open. Calvin strolled out with open arms and a wide grin, saying, "There she is."

She practically skipped over and gave him a big fat smooch on the lips. Must've been the boss man's new girlfriend, cuz this woman was a hell of a lot younger and darker-skinned than Missus Lenard.

"Did you meet Tristian?" He broadly gestured in my direction. "This here's my most reliable employee."

If that's true, you need to replace your whole staff. All two of 'em.

"Nice to meet you," said the woman. "I'm Vidya."

I mumbled some kind of greeting.

"You mind keeping watch for a while?" Calvin said. "We're gonna go out and grab some lunch."

By that he meant go to a motel and fuck her brains out.

"Sure," I said. "Have fun."

The door chimed shut behind Calvin and his girlfriend. The liquor store was clean and empty. We'd been open for an hour, so the daily alkies had already come and gone. Weekdays were always slow. I leaned back in the chair, interlaced my fingers behind my head, and summoned all my strength not to take a nap.

Twenty minutes later, a pair of men burst through the door and ran to the counter. They wore hoods over their heads and black medical masks with sunglasses to conceal their faces. I stood up, and before I could do or say anything, a pair of pistols were hovering over the cash register. The barrels were black, like a predator's eyes.

"Hand over the fuckin' money," barked the bigger man. "The register *and* the safe."

I glanced at the door, half expecting Calvin and his date to meander back inside at just the wrong moment.

"I can give you the register," I said. "But I don't know the combo to the safe."

That was a lie, but I might as well give it a shot. The bigger man cussed. His accomplice hopped over the counter and emptied the register into an unzipped backpack worn backward against his chest for easy access. The big guy stormed across the store and knocked over racks of snacks as he went. He found the door marked **PRIVATE** and started kicking under the doorknob. It was a sturdy door, and it showed no signs of giving way.

The accomplice called out to the lead man, "There's only eighty fuckin' dollars in here, man."

The big guy stopped kicking. He doubled over, hyperventilating, and said between breaths, "Help me with this door."

"This is taking too long. Let's split."

The big guy kicked the **PRIVATE** door again, and there was a loud snap. But the door didn't budge. He yelped and tumbled to the floor, and I covered my mouth so they wouldn't see me laughing. The accomplice ran over and said, "What the fuck's the matter?"

"I think I just broke something. Let's get the hell out of here."

They grabbed all the booze they could carry on their way out: a six-pack of Coors and a couple handles of cheap tequila. The door chimed in the breeze, swinging and slowly coming to a rest.

"Jesus Christ a-fuckin'-live," I said.

I got my phone out of my pocket and instinctively dialed 911. Then I thought better of that and called Calvin. He picked up on the first ring of the second call, sounding pretty goddamn annoyed.

"What?"

"Some assholes just knocked the place over. You might wanna call Annie."

He hung up without saying anything. I locked the doors and swung the sign to the closed side. It was an excruciating ten minutes waiting for Calvin to show up. He'd sent his girlfriend home, and he had called the Vietnamese mob and told them to send Annie.

Anh "Annie" Phan was the daughter of the local boss, and she played a role you might expect from an oldest son: heir, ambassador, and fist of the boss all rolled together. She wore sharp suits and very little makeup — just enough to look sleek but nothing too titillating — and she wore her shoulder-length black hair in a thin ponytail that reminded me of that guy Furio from *The Sopranos*.

Her accomplice was a massive beast called Adrien who looked like he could be a sumo wrestler, if only he was Japanese. Six-foot-three with a ridiculous wingspan, he was built like a Dick Tracy mob boss. It wasn't clear how much of him was fat and how much was muscle, but if anyone could lift you by the throat or crush your trachea with one hand, it was this guy. He wore a loose tracksuit over his massive form, which must've been at least 4XL if not a custom job.

I stood with Calvin in the parking lot. Annie had her eyes laser-focused on us, reading our body language for any little tell. Adrien stood behind her holding something in the pocket of his track jacket.

"So what happened?" she said. "Start from the start."

I saw no use in lying. I genuinely had no idea who the fuck these guys were. They didn't press me about the safe code, so they clearly didn't know what they were doing. Annie and Adrien seemed especially interested in locating the big guy with a big mouth and a bum foot.

Annie looked at Calvin and said, "So you just happened to be out on a date, huh?"

"It was lunchtime," Calvin said. "We didn't have reservations. We just went out."

She stared him down and said nothing. Something in his tone gave him away. I wasn't sure what it was, but if I felt it, and that meant Annie felt it too.

"Thanks," she said. "We'll take it from here." She gestured to her massive enforcer and said, "Let's go."

Annie hopped behind the wheel of her little sports car, and the big muscle guy struggled to squeeze into the passenger seat. They squealed tires and peeled off.

"Jesus," I muttered. "Hate to be those guys."

Calvin didn't say anything. He just went back inside, and I followed.

"Where's Vidya?"

"She went home," Calvin said. "Listen. Thanks for being reliable."

"What do you mean?"

"The safe." He shrugged. "I mean, the register was bad enough. Imagine I had to explain that?"

"I didn't do a fuckin' thing. They just ran in and stuck their guns in my face. I said I didn't know the combo, and they believed me."

"All right, relax," Calvin said. "I'm just saying, most guys would've given up as soon as they saw a pair of gats. I appreciate you not doing that."

"Well, I appreciate your appreciation."

"Don't get cunty with me." He pulled his wallet out of his pocket and whipped out two hundred-dollar bills. "It's not just gratitude I wanna give ya."

"I don't need the money," I said.

"Then whoever walks in next can have it." He slapped the bills on the counter and went back to the door marked **PRIVATE**. He slammed the door and locked it shut.

A pair of college kids came into the shop and started riffling through the beer fridge and snack racks. Probably stocking up for a party. I took the money off the counter before they could come by and see it for themselves.

ON THE MORNING of the VIP game, I felt worse than ever. I was hung over as shit, and I'd barely slept a wink. Every time I drifted into restfulness, I had a dream about being tied to a chair and a huge sumo douchebag snarling in my face with a dog's rotten breath. I woke up sweating every forty minutes or so.

I shambled into work three minutes after eleven with the enthusiasm of a gulag prisoner. The queue of alkies waited outside, kicking rocks and looking impatient and mad as hell.

"For fuck's sake," said a bearded old man. "Someone's finally here."

"Nobody opened?" I said.

"No," the alkies said in unison. I unlocked the door and went inside, then I hit the lights. Nothing was out of the ordinary, except the place was empty. The alkies hurried in after me, and I was too distracted to stop them or say anything.

"Hey," one of them complained. "The fridges are still locked."

"Give me a fuckin' minute," I said.

I approached the **PRIVATE** door with the caution of a gunslinger entering an outlaw's hideout. Like a badman with a gun might rush out and blast me in the gut. I reached for the knob and tried to turn it, but it was locked. Then I let out a breath.

"Lemme get those fridges for you," I said.

The liquor store went quiet once the alkies had been served and went on their way. I approached Calvin's office again and pressed my ear against the door. There was nothing to hear, as far as I could tell. But Calvin was supposed to be here today. Where the hell was he?

Forty minutes after noon, my good friend Andrew Chapman showed up to get his once-every-so-often fix of booze. He grabbed a six-pack from the fridge and leaned against the counter next to the register. Then he glanced around and said, "Now a good time to talk?"

"Sure," I said. "The cameras don't have any sound. Just don't look suspicious."

Andrew chuckled nervously. He paid for his beers and then went ahead and cracked one. Then he offered me a beer, and I said something about professional duties and whatnot. But we both knew that was a bunch of bullshit, so I cracked a beer and drank it with him.

"What'd you wanna talk about?"

"This thing tonight," Andrew said. "It's not worth it. Let's bail."

"What are you talking about? Everything's lined up. You don't want Calvin to get killed, do you?"

"Of course I don't. Shit, I dunno." He shrugged and scratched his neck and looked around. Anything to avoid looking me in the eyes. "It just feels like I'm taking all the risk, and you're doing jack shit."

"Are you fucking kidding me? All you gotta do is stick a plastic gun in Joey's face and take his bag. I'm the one who's gotta talk to the fuckin' mob guys. If I make any sorta slip-up, even tiniest fuckin' error, they're gonna rip my ass apart. If you wanna switch jobs, I'm happy."

"Relax," Andrew said. "I was just thinking out loud."

We sipped our beers and glanced around. Everything was quiet today, but the crowd always picked up once the second tier of alkies finished lunch and showed up to score their daily potion.

"Look," I said. "If you're so fuckin' worried about Joey recognizing you, why don't you just use a voice mod or some shit?"

"That'd just make it more obvious it's someone he knows," Andrew said.

"Or just don't say anything. Let your gun do the talking."

"You want me to shoot him?"

"No," I said. "Don't shoot him, you fuckin' idiot. Then he'll know it's fake. I mean shove it in his face, give him the right idea."

"I'm starting to regret this. You better be out there watching my back when this goes down."

"What, you want a witness? It's better if it's just you and Joey. Then it's his word and nobody else's."

"If you say so."

We finished our beers, and I fist-bumped Andrew and he took off. Calvin came into work half an hour later, sputtering some nonsense about a family emergency. He shuffled back into his office and locked the door behind him. I kicked back in my chair and burned the day away waiting for something to happen.

The sky was gray, and it had started to rain. The day passed by, and almost nobody showed up except a few alcoholic regulars at their scheduled runtime. It was a bunch of bullshit, and we all knew it. The only reason I had a living wage was because robots weren't up to the task yet. Give it another ten or twenty years, and people like me were gonna be on the street.

It made me sick thinking about it. In a just world, I'd've been born to the kind of generational wealth where you never have to work a day in your life. Imagine that kind of life. Maybe you work here and there, if you really feel like it. But at the end of the day, life is just a series of personal preferences. If you prefer not to work, nothing will ever compel you to do so.

And there I thought: in a few days, that could be my life. I wouldn't be a multimillionaire, but if the score were as big as Joey'd said, then I'd never need to work again.

The day was crawling by slowly. It felt like evening, but it was only half past three. Joey showed up for his shift, thirty minutes late. Not that I cared one way or another.

"Hey, man," I said.

Joey ignored me. No remark or nod, not even an odd sneer. He just walked right past me without looking at me. In one of those weird moods today. I didn't mind. I felt that way too from time to time.

An elderly couple shuffled into the shop and made their way to the liquor aisles. Joey came out of the bathroom and scoffed at them when he passed. They didn't seem to notice, or maybe they didn't care. He came around behind the counter and dropped into the chair next to me.

"Jesus, man," I said. "What's your problem?"

"What?"

"Why are you acting all pissy?"

Joey scoffed and didn't say anything. He took out his phone and started texting someone. The elderly man came over and plopped down a pair of 750 ml bottles of Jose Cuervo, and his hunchback wife followed along with her cane in one hand and a ceramic Clase Azul cradled in the other arm.

I snickered and said, "Check this out."

Joey ignored me. The wife shuffled up to the counter and gently set the fine Clase Azul next to the bottles of distilled mule piss. I rang them up and made some small talk like I normally did.

"How you folks doing?"

"Good," the man said in a raspy voice.

"We're gonna party tonight," croaked the old woman.

It took everything in my being not to burst out laughing. I pursed my lips and mumbled something incoherent — even I didn't know what I said. Twenty bucks for each Cuervo and two hundred for the Clase Azul.

"That'll be two-eighty-three and thirty cents," I sputtered.

The old man paid with his debit card. I bagged up their stuff, the Joses in a paper grocery bag and the Case Azul carefully wrapped like a gift, and they thanked me and went on their way. When the door swung shut behind them, I burst out laughing and dropped back into my chair.

"That was fuckin' funny."

"What was?" Joey said.

"Did you see what they were buying? The guy got two bottles of total crap, but his wife bought some *really* good stuff."

"They bought it together. Maybe they're for both of them."

"Sure, I mean. You're prolly right." My face went hot red, and I forced another chuckle. "Anyway, it's whatever. We all good for tonight?"

He scoffed again and didn't say anything. I waited and said, "So is that a yes or a no?"

"Remember that thing you suggested?"

"What thing?"

"Get shitfaced, fuck a couple call girls, go down the freeway. You remember that?"

I opened my mouth and couldn't speak. Then I squeaked out the words, "Not really."

"Well, I've been thinking about it. And yeah. I think we're good for tonight."

"Sure, man."

In truth, I did know what he was talking about. I remembered saying we could get shitfaced, fuck some hookers, and go down the freeway. But that story ended with our heads plastered to the concrete divider, and I didn't think I was serious when I made that suggestion.

I cleared my throat and said, "What exactly are we talking about here?"

"What?"

"You know," I said. "With the suicide thing."

"Suicide?" Joey said. "What the fuck are you talking about?"

"Going down the freeway."

"Yeah," Joey said. "Drive down the freeway. Get some wind in our hair. Maybe hit a casino. What were you talking about?"

"Nothing," I said. "Never mind."

6

WE DIDN'T EXCHANGE a single word for the rest of the shift. I got off an hour later and left Joey to close shop. The vibes were getting real bad. Not that Joey was a chill guy by any means, but everything about him was edgier than usual. I kicked back on the couch and watched a poker game in Vegas. One guy was wearing sunglasses and a blazer, and the other wore a t-shirt and jeans. The guy in the blazer was getting cleaned out. Someone called my cell phone, and I picked up and answered.

"Yeah?"

"It's me," Andrew said. "What's good?"

"I'm just chilling. Wanna come through?"

"No, I mean. What's good with tonight?"

"We're ready to go. Joey's gonna call me when they're wrapping up."

"And you know for a fact it's gonna be Sunday at nine?"

I pinched the bridge of my nose and said, "Not exactly. It could be any time. But it's gonna be Sunday night, for sure."

"So what, I just gotta clear my whole schedule?"

"I mean, ideally — yeah. Fuck me, I'll handle it myself."

A sigh came down the line. "Fine. I'll be ready."

Saturday came and went in a foggy haze. I manned the shop with Calvin and a high school kid of about fifteen years. The boss of the Viet mob, Minh "Dennis" Phan, didn't just own Calvin's Liquors — he also owned the coffee shop down the street where they held VIP games. Dennis felt bad depriving Calvin of a core employee like Joey Patrone, so he sent his nephew to work an "internship" at the liquor store. Basically that meant free child labor on the downlow.

"Is this even legal?" I muttered.

Calvin scoffed and said, "Hell if I know. But it's what Dennis said, so fuck it."

He sauntered back into his office and locked the **PRIVATE** door behind him. I dropped behind the register. The kid was sitting in Joey's usual chair. We waited in silence while nothing happened. It was half past noon, and the game wouldn't wrap up until tomorrow evening. I tapped my foot like it might pass the time better.

"You mind if I play with my Switch?" the kid blurted out.

"Your what?"

"It's a handheld." He pulled a small black case out of his backpack and zipped it open, revealing a little handheld gaming console. I wasn't much of a gamer, but I'd heard of this thing.

"Sure, man," I said. "Have fun."

The kid fired up his Switch and started playing some game where he was running around in a suit of armor fighting enormous monsters. I crossed my feet on the counter and opened up a book. *Art of the Deal* was today's reading. I was never a fan of ol' Don, but these days I started to see his appeal.

Sunday was much the same. A valve in my system cranked up and released a shit-ton of adrenaline. I couldn't sit still, and I spent the whole day walking around the store straightening out stock and rearranging things. Even the kid could tell something was wrong, but he didn't say much. He just sat there playing with his Switch, eyeing me every now and then like I might grab a bottle at any moment and launch it at his head.

I walked out to the sidewalk and lit up a cigarette. The day was cold, cloudy, and gray. Just like yesterday. Maybe tomorrow would be different. I sucked the stoge and blew a hefty plume of smoke. An urge pumped through my veins like a shot of heroin, telling me to get on my phone and call Andrew right now. Call it all off, tell him to stay home. But the urge faded, and I was left standing there in the high of its fading, a cigarette dangling from my lips while I watched rain gather in the sky. Some drizzle touched my face, so I stomped out the cigarette and went back inside.

The sun went down, and it was getting late. Around eight thirty, the kid packed up his Switch and said his mom was there to pick him up. I nodded and didn't say anything. I had the place all to myself after he left. I shivered and waited. Every few minutes I had to stand up and air my ass out, I was so goddamn sweaty.

At ten thirty, half an hour before closing time, I stood up behind the counter and stretched my arms behind my shoulders. Then I glanced at my phone. No word yet from Joey.

Eleven o'clock. I locked the front door and sat back behind the counter with my book. But I couldn't concentrate. I'd barely read two pages all day long. I went out back and smoked another quick cigarette in the parking lot, but it didn't do much to calm me down.

So I sat inside and waited. I started worrying about this and that. For one thing, the cameras were still rolling in the shop. If anyone checked the reel, they'd see me pacing around like a freshman waiting for his first date. So I took a deep breath and kicked my feet up on the counter like usual, trying my best to look relaxed. But we all know that's a paradox — you can't *try* to chill out. You just do.

Two minutes before midnight, I got a text. It was fortuitous I saw it when I did, since I'd been nodding off behind the counter, sleeping fifteen minutes here and there, and I almost dozed again before the buzz of the phone woke me up.

It was a message from Joey. *We're wrapping up*, it said. *Be there soon.*

Now seemed like a decent time to call Andrew and make sure everything was good to go. But the cameras would catch me making the call, and that'd look suspicious. Not to mention there's ways to retrieve a call log, even if you delete the history from your phone. So I thought better of it. I stood up and yawned and stretched. Better to get the blood flowing rather than to fall back asleep.

Minutes passed in silence. I paced feverishly behind the counter, cold and sweaty and nauseous all at once. Things outside were completely still, and I couldn't see anything in the dark through the glass front door. Maybe I should sit down so it would look less suspicious when—

The door flung open, and Joey stormed inside. His face was bright red and his veins bulged. He didn't say anything, just marched straight at me.

"Hey, man," I said. "What's wrong?"

Joey grabbed me by the collar and socked me in the gut. Then he pressed me against the wall. His breath reeked of cigarettes with a touch of Champagne.

"You motherfucker," he shrieked. "What'd you do, huh?"

I coughed my lungs out. Son of a bitch had knocked the wind out of me, and I was sure he'd kill me right there. I did my best to fight back, but I was too weak to do anything. He clenched my shirt like his life depended on it.

"Get off me," I said.

"What the fuck did you do?"

"Nothing," I shouted. Finally, I broke free from Joey's grip, and he stumbled back snarling like a rabid animal. He even had a bit of mad-dog foam dribbling down his chin. I said, "What the fuck happened, man?"

"We need to get out of here," Joey said. He paced around just short of a jog. "Wait, no. We need to call Annie. Get her ass on the phone right now."

"You gonna tell me what happened?" I said.

"*Get her on the phone.*"

"What do I tell her?"

Joey grabbed my shirt again and growled, "We just got robbed."

They showed up in ten minutes flat. Annie wore a full black suit with a white shirt, red tie, and a thin white cotton scarf that draped down her shoulders. Her enormous associate came in behind her in his usual tracksuit getup. We followed them out back into the empty parking lot, where she and Adrien stood opposite of us cowering men. She took out a pack of cigarettes and offered us one. Neither of us accepted.

At this point, I was ready to puke. I'd been pretty confident in my plans that Joey would take the chop, and everybody else — including me — would be spared from any violence. When I saw those eyes, I knew right away I'd been wrong. They weren't angry at all. In fact, her demeanor wasn't any different than our last meeting, when we talked about an armed robbery that cost the store $83.

It didn't totally crystalize yet, but that was the first time I knew what people really meant when they talked about feeling the walls close in on them.

Annie lit up her cigarette and got started. "So. What's the rundown?"

"I was at the game since Friday," Joey said. "It just wrapped up, I dunno, twenty minutes ago. Your boy, that Charles Bronson-looking guy, he counted the cash in the back room with his associates. Then he came out, gave me an envelope, and I walked back here."

Annie stared him down and waited for him to continue. This was perfect. *Look as suspicious as you can, you stupid motherfucker. When the axe comes down, let it be your ass on the line and not mine or Calvin's.*

"So anyway," Joey continued, "I didn't get twenty fuckin' steps before some asshole came up behind me. He didn't say shit to me, just fuckin' beat me over the head and tased me. He must've known about the envelope, 'cause he rooted through my coat and took it right away. Didn't even bother with my fuckin' wallet."

A black mark crossed over my soul. If I'd been less careful, Annie might've noticed my eyes drop. Or maybe she did notice. That stupid goddamn motherfucker, Andrew, was supposed to announce himself. Make it look like a random but highly unlucky robbery. Now they'd know for a fact it was an inside job.

Annie blew a puff of smoke and said, "What else?"

"That's pretty much it," Joey said. "Once I got on my feet, I ran back here. We called you right away."

She looked at me and said, "What about you? Got anything to add?"

"I've just been working all day," I said. "We closed at eleven, but I hung around 'cause we were gonna go hit the club after Joey got off working your game."

She cocked an eye at me.

"Game?" Annie said with an incredulous smile. "What game?"

My chest raced and adrenaline pumped. I tried to think of something smart to say, some slick way to recover, but nothing came to mind. I hung my mouth open until Joey chimed in. "I told him I've been working a game these last few nights. We're roommates. It helps to stay in the loop."

Looking interested, she grinned and said, "Roommates, huh?"

"Not *that* kind of roommate," he sputtered. "We just live together. I was gonna be gone for a few days, so I didn't want him filing a missing person report."

We both laughed nervously, and Annie just exchanged her stare between the two of us. A moment of quiet passed, and she let us squirm.

"How much do you think got stolen tonight?" Annie said. Joey and I stared blankly at her. "Just a wild guess. What do you think?"

"Well," Joey shrugged, "there were a lot of VIPs there tonight. High rollers and shit. They were spinning ten-thousand dollar chips like fuckin' tops, so I'd guess two mil at least."

She dropped her half-finished cigarette and stomped it on the asphalt with the flat of her heel.

"Listen," she said. "This is what's gonna happen. We're gonna be hands-off on this thing, but we expect that money back soon. Make sense?"

I felt like I'd swallowed a cinder block.

"So uh," Joey said, "how much time do we have?"

She shrugged with a little grimace and said, "Y'know. The usual."

"The usual," Joey said with a dark expression. "You mean, like, vig and all?"

"Vig and all."

Annie gestured to her huge friend, and they walked around the side of the liquor store and headed back to their car parked out front. We stood there in the frigid night and listened to the engine rev before they drove off. The moon and stars glowed in the endless black sky. I looked up at the cosmos and wondered if death was like staring into a sky with no stars.

"Fuck me," Joey growled. He stormed back inside, and I waited out there contemplating the universe.

WE WENT HOME and drank enough to kill a horse. It took all my strength and willpower to keep myself from blacking out. Once Joey was comatose on the couch, I dialed Andrew and paced around.

"Yeah," came his voice on the line.

"Hey, man." I grinned. "Let's meet up."

"It's four in the fuckin' morning. I'm still at work."

I cackled and said, "Work? You gotta be shitting me. We never gotta work again after this."

Panic overwhelmed me. The humiliated kind of panic where you realize you just made a dire and unavoidable mistake. I glanced back at Joey, thinking he'd be on his feet with a gun drawn on me.

But he was still blacked out on the couch. I crept back into my bedroom and shut the door, then I whispered into my phone. "I'll swing by and pick up my take."

Andrew didn't argue with me. I hopped in my car and drove through the drizzling night to the cemetery across town where he worked a night shift. I parked the car in the lot and shut off the engine. My headlights stayed on, and I could see old graves beyond the iron gate, casting long shadows into the darkness.

Andrew came out of a security hut and beelined over to the passenger side of my car.

"It's freakin' cold tonight," I said when he dropped in and shut the door.

"You fucked up," he said. There was a certain shakiness in his voice that guaranteed he wasn't kidding.

I looked at him and said, "What?"

"There wasn't two million dollars, you stupid fucking dumbass."

"But Annie just said—"

"There was only ninety-five *thousand*."

My mouth hung open and my eyes were like circles. I yelped, "*What?*"

"You heard me," Andrew said.

"All right, relax. What the fuck are you talking about? What happened?"

"It went down like you said. I held him up, and I told him to hand over his wallet. He didn't say shit, he just reached for his gun. So I fuckin' tased him, and I took the envelope from his jacket."

"Is that how it went down?" I said plainly.

"Yeah," he said. "I was scared shitless. I thought he was gonna kill me."

I couldn't think of anything to say that I wanted him to hear.

"What?" Andrew said.

"Nothing. So when you got home, you looked in the envelope and that's all there was. Ninety-five fuckin' thousand."

"That's the long and short of it."

I buried my face in my hands and said, "You gotta be fucking shitting me."

"What happened with those chink mobsters? Did they kill Joey yet?"

"No," I said. "They didn't kill anyone."

Andrew's expression turned sour. "What do you mean?"

"I mean nobody's dead. They told Joey to get the money back."

"Aw, great," Andrew said. "That's just great."

"Relax," I said. "It's no biggie."

"Yeah, it's not your ass on the line. He's gonna come find me, dude. He's gonna find my fuckin' family, all over your measly-ass ninety-five thousand—"

I shouted down his bubbling panic. "Take it easy. He's not gonna find you. I'm gonna cover for you."

"How? You gonna let some sorry asshole take the blame?"

"Actually," I smirked, "we've got a red herring already lined up."

"Who?"

"Gilbert Rodriguez. You remember that guy from high school?"

"Sorta," Andrew said. "Not really. Was he at the store the other day?"

"Yeah."

"Why him?"

"He runs with that lowlife crew," I said. "Asked me to steal stock. Shit, man, they were prolly the guys who held me up the other day. We could pin it on 'em easy."

"I thought the point of this was to *stop* people from getting hurt."

I couldn't find anything reasonable to say to that.

"Whatever," Andrew mumbled. "It's too late now, I guess."

"It's best I leave you out of the details. The less you know, the better. Anyway, you wanna grab a couple drinks?"

"No, I wanna finish my shift and go home."

"Hold up," I said. "Where's my half?"

"It's at my house. I'll drop it off tomorrow."

Andrew stepped out of the car and slammed the door shut. He pulled his hood over his head and hurried back to the security hut. A cold shiver washed over me. Right in that moment, I'd never felt lonelier. I'd gone through with a horrible thing, and I had no money or friends to show for it.

The next morning, I dragged myself out of my bedroom and stalked through the apartment as cautious as a burglar. Like something hostile might be waiting for me.

I saw nothing. Joey wasn't on the couch where he'd been asleep last night, and he wasn't in his room either. He was gone for the day. Our roommate, Marianne, was in the kitchen frying up some eggs. I sauntered past her and went out the front door in the same stinking outfit I'd slept in.

When I parked in the lot behind Calvin's, I hauled myself out of the car with the enthusiasm of a hemorrhoid patient making his way to a stable. The back door was unlocked, and the room was still dark. Joey was supposed to open today. Did he leave without locking? Or maybe he just stepped out for a couple minutes.

I unlocked the fridges and pressed my face against the glass front door. Nobody was waiting out front. Another anomaly, given the morning alkies came by every day as sure as the sun rises. I checked the time on my phone: 10:55 a.m. *Fuck it,* I thought. *Might as well open up.*

There was an awful putrid stench out front, and it came from a blue cooler sitting next to the door. I covered my mouth with my elbow.

The pieces were right in front of me, so to speak, but I couldn't put them together. Maybe it was an act of willful ignorance, or maybe I'm just plain stupid. I swung open the cooler lid, and Calvin Lenard's pale face poked back at me from the red ice. He was locked in an expression of empty shock, with plastic eyes and a frozen tongue. Chopped-up Popsicle limbs stuck out of the ice on either side of him.

Right then, it became clear just how fucked we were.

Part Three — Ante Up

7

THIS WASN'T THE KIND OF THING we could handle in-house, so I called the police right away. Whoever killed Calvin had left him there as a message or a warning or something. What was I supposed to do, hide the body myself?

A patrol officer showed up, asked me some preliminary questions, then hung around the scene to keep things safe until the big boys arrived. A black Town Car rolled up and parked in the street in front of Calvin's Liquors. A woman stepped out of the driver seat wearing blue jeans and a hoodless sweater with big yellow letters across the chest that read *SJPD*. She was practically bald with her thin buzz cut.

She approached me and nodded at the patrolman, who went back to his cruiser and took off. She extended a hand to me and introduced herself.

"I'm Detective Lieutenant Erin King," she said. "Here on behalf of San Jose's finest."

"Tristian Sloan." I shook her hand.

In her wake followed an ambulance and a van full of technicians, analysts, and interns who took away the cooler and started gathering fingerprints and footprints and hair molecules from all over the scene. Detective King put her hand on my shoulder and led me away so the team could perform their work undisturbed. We walked down the sidewalk, and she asked more questions.

"First of all," she said, "I'm really sorry for your loss. I understand you worked directly with the victim. Were you close?"

"Close?" I said. "No. He was kind of an asshole, but he was an all-right guy."

"I know how that is. I've mourned plenty assholes in my time. Did you notice anything suspicious in the hours or days leading up to the discovery?"

"What do you mean, strange?"

"Anything at all that stood out to you as unusual," she said. "Strangers loitering around. Calvin stepping out for odd calls. Anything at all."

"Well, we got held up a few days ago."

"Yeah, we know about that. I understand the lead investigator's doing his best. Anything else?"

"Not that I can think of."

"And your coworker, Joseph Patrone. Where is he right now?"

"I have no idea. Haven't seen him since last night."

Detective King nodded. She stared me in the eyes with laser-like precision that intended to scorch through any doubt or deception.

"If you have a card or something, I can give it to him next time I see him."

"Sure," said Detective King. "You do that."

There was nothing I could give up without killing myself one way or the other. If I turned the blame on Annie and Adrien, Dennis Phan would send someone to settle the score. Maybe Joey could take the heat instead, but then everyone would know I was a rat, and the outcome wouldn't be much different one way or another.

Then there was Gilbert. The cops must have a line on his crew after that first robbery. Maybe they'll get lazy and pin it on all him.

Anyway, the detective left with jack shit. The van full of technicians and analysts asked me questions about next of kin before they left to file Calvin away at the morgue. His poor wife and kids would have to go claim his remains. Or maybe it'd be his mistress, depending on who was close enough these days to handle the paperwork.

Once they were gone, I locked up the store and turned the **CLOSED** sign. Then I sat behind the counter and fished around for my secret stash, a gap between the countertop and support beam, perfectly suited to hide an eighth of weed along with a small pipe. I packed myself a bowl and grabbed a lighter from the BIC stand on the counter.

There was no point in hiding it from the camera now. Nobody was gonna chew me out. I lit up the bowl and took a rip. The harshness surprised me. Normally I used a bong, where the smoke gets nicely filtered through some stale black water.

It was too fucked-up for me to think about. Why'd they kill Calvin? It was so goddamn senseless. I sauntered over to the fridges and grabbed a six-pack of IPAs, then I set them on the counter and opened a bottle. Someone tried to enter the liquor store, but the door lock stopped them. They knocked on the glass.

It was just about the last person I expected to see standing behind that glass door. She gave me a sheepish smile and said muffled through the door, "You guys open?"

"Of course," I said.

The store reeked of weed, and a layer of white smoke hung over everything. Rachel noted it right away when I let her in, but she didn't seem to mind.

"Mind if I get a hit?" she said.

"Sure."

I led her behind the counter, and we sat down together on the uncomfortable folding chairs. I packed a fresh bowl and handed her the pipe and the lighter. She lit it up and blew a puff of smoke.

"Isn't your boss kind of a dick?" she said. "How come he's letting you smoke now?"

I didn't reply.

Rachel handed over the pipe and the lighter, but I put up my palm. I never liked the taste of a half-smoked bowl. She finished it off and started coughing.

"Prolly too soon to make the news," I said in a low voice.

"What?"

I told her everything. Way more than I'd intended. It all just spilled right out of me, and I wanted to sob on her shoulder, but if I did that, I might die from the humiliation. I even told her about the fucking VIP game.

She stared at me with unblinking eyes, agape. She clearly had no idea what to say.

"I know," I said. "It was a dumbass move."

"So why are you still here?"

"What, like, still alive?"

"You're grieving," she said. "You should take the day off. Hell, maybe a whole week."

"I dunno," I said.

But really, I did know. We gathered up a hoard of beer and tequila, then I closed the store and we headed home. It was real nerve-wracking opening my apartment door, not knowing if Joey was on the other side, I can tell you that much. But our place was just as I'd left it this morning.

"Where's Joey?" Rachel said.

I didn't reply. I walked to the fridge and shoved the beers inside and then grabbed some clean glasses from the cupboard. There weren't any shot glasses left, so I grabbed some dinner cups like you'd use to drink milk, then I filled them up with tequila.

When we finished fucking, we cuddled together on the couch and watched TV in our underwear. Rachel said, "What if someone comes home?"

"Whatever," I said. "Joey's seen me in my underwear."

She raised a brow and said, "Has he?"

"Not like that. We're roommates."

"What about the other one? Marianne or whatever."

"She mostly just stays with her boyfriend."

"I see."

We smoked and drank together until we were as useless as we were happy. For a little while I forgot all about the worries that eroded my mind. I couldn't believe Calvin was gone. It was real fuckin' obvious who did it, and it pissed me off I couldn't do anything about it. You'd need a John Wick type of guy to take on the Viet mob.

A few hours later, the lock clicked and the door swung open. Marianne came into the living room and froze when she saw us on the couch together. We woke up stunned, Rachel mortified and apologizing her lungs out while we frantically dressed ourselves.

I felt like I hadn't slept in weeks. We went to a tropical-themed bar in downtown San Jose, and we crushed drinks like it was Friday night. Truthfully, I had no idea what day it was. I was more interested in numbing the pain than keeping track of silly things like the day and time.

I didn't sleep the next night either, lying awake all night next to Rachel in the bed at her place. The sun peered through the window and woke her up like a natural alarm. She got up and started getting dressed, and by some ironic twist of fate I finally started falling asleep before she nudged me in the ribs and said, "Come on. Get up."

"What," I moaned.

"You gotta go."

"What, is your boyfriend home?"

"Not my boyfriend. My partner."

I gave Rachel a cockeyed stare that was half confused and half asleep.

"We have an arrangement," she explained. "And that means you gotta go."

She escorted me out of the apartment. When we passed the kitchen, I tried to get a good look at this partner of hers. It wasn't clear who exactly I was looking for, and I knew it would hurt either way, but I just needed to know if it was a man or a woman who'd won her affection over me.

As far as I could tell, Rachel's partner was a lesbian. You know the type, short-haired with a fine figure but a weird haircut with dye tips and a fuckin' attitude toward anyone who's not another hot lesbian. They always pissed me off. Fuck them.

Rachel ushered me out the front door and tried to shut it behind me. I grabbed the door and pried it open, then I leaned in and whispered to her.

"What happened?" I said. "I thought we had something."

"I thought we did, too," she said. "But you didn't wanna get tied down."

"Who the hell's she?"

"She's my friend."

I furrowed my brows with a look that told her to come on, tell me the truth.

"My friend with benefits," she admitted. "Look, you left me all fired up that night. So I went out and met her. What'd you expect?"

I let go of the door, and she slammed it in my face.

Once I left her apartment complex, I realized the world's biggest dumbass had left my car parked downtown. Somehow that seemed to track. Rachel might've been down to give me a ride if I apologized for being a dick and asked really nicely. But I couldn't stand the humiliation of going back in there. So I sighed, stuck my hands in my pockets, and started toward the nearest bus stop.

My place was still empty when I got back. No sign of Joey since last night. I went to my bedroom and found my cellphone where I'd forgotten it yesterday. There were three-dozen missed calls from Andrew.

He answered halfway through the first ring and said, "Hey man, what the fuck? You scared the shit out of me."

"Sorry." I chuckled. "I was out late. Left my phone at home."

"Lemme drop off your half. Where do you wanna meet?"

I checked the time. It was a quarter past eleven. The morning alkies had probably moved on by now.

"Come swing by the liquor store," I said. "I'm running late anyways."

I MET UP WITH ANDREW outside the cameras' view in the rear lot. Andrew parked across three empty spaces and left his engine running, and I sauntered over and dropped into the passenger seat.

"What's good, man?" I said.

"What the fuck happened to Calvin?" he growled.

I let out a heavy breath and said, "Someone got him."

"No shit. Who got him, the chinks?"

"I dunno. Could've been anyone."

Andrew laughed without a shred of humor, and there was existential panic brimming in his eyes. "No," he said. "It couldn't of."

"So what's your theory?"

"My *theory?*" Andrew shouted. "Obviously the fuckin' gooks did it."

"Relax, man. Lower your goddamn voice, and watch the fuckin' pejoratives."

"What are you, a goddamn liberal now? Do you realize how fucked-up this is? The only way this could've gone any worse if they were playing with Monopoly money."

"It's under control," I said. "Me and Joey, we talked to the Viet mob. They're laying back."

"Why?"

Here came the difficult part, selling this to Andrew without him flipping his shit. I rubbed my chin, and that act of nervous hesitation was enough to set him off.

"*Why,*" he yelled.

"Me and Joey are on point with this thing."

"What thing?"

"You know." I let out a tense breath. "Getting the money back."

Andrew was fuming red. It must've been an act of Herculean strength to keep himself from screaming his head off. Instead he just quietly said, "What?"

I threw up my hands and laid it out for him. "They want me and Joey to track down the money."

"Well, that's just great." Andrew laughed, but it was the kind of laugh when you're in a serious panic and don't know what else to do. "What the fuck, man? I thought you had my back."

"Dude, relax," I said. "Your name's not gonna come up. You're gonna be fine."

"They're gonna be looking at the regulars. People like me. They could find my family."

"Nobody's finding your family, man. Chill the fuck out, all right? I'm on point with this, and I've got it under control."

"How?"

I didn't really want to tell Andrew this part of the plan. He was a civilian, much like me, and this part was a little gritty for either of our liking. But fuck it, I had to tell him something so he'd quit panicking. Once a guy starts to panic, it's not long before he decides maybe talking to the cops isn't such a bad idea after all.

"We've got a fall guy," I said with a tense breath.

"Yeah, you told me that. How's that gonna work?"

"Don't worry about it." I patted Andrew on the shoulder, and the man returned a mean stare. "I've got Joey under control. Just take it easy. We're gonna reopen Calvin's in a day or two, once Dennis gets his shit together and figures out who's running it. Then you can come by like usual and pick up your Sierra Nevadas."

"That seems like a bad move," Andrew muttered.

"What are you talking about? You can't go and change up your daily routine. They'll notice."

"Whatever," Andrew said. "Your take's in the glovebox."

I took out the manila envelope and counted the wad of cash. It contained forty-seven thousand and five hundred dollars. Precisely half the take. I looked at it and sighed.

"Something wrong?" Andrew said.

"It's so small." I took out the wad of cash and stuffed it into my hip pocket, then I dropped the envelope on the floor. "There, you can keep that."

I slammed the car door shut and Andrew peeled away. I went back inside and manned my position behind the counter. It was quiet, cold, and grey. The fridges were frosted over like someone had turned the temperature down too low. I couldn't help but shiver. The cool clouds of condensation and bits of ice reminded me of that cooler full of Calvin parts. Every time I closed my eyes, I saw his wax-frozen face staring blankly at oblivion.

Nothing could shake it — I felt horrible. Maybe all this could've been avoided if I'd just done the Johnny Citizen thing and gone to the police. But what would I tell them? My gangster friend wants to rob his gangster boss? Next thing I knew, they'd have me wearing a wire. Fuck that.

It didn't matter now. Calvin was already dead.

I jerked forward and dry-heaved. There was nothing in my stomach to puke up. I just sat there with my hand on the counter, and my world spun in a dizzy haze.

The door jingled, and a pair of *Jersey Shore*-looking guys came in with bright shirts and bad tans. I pounded my chest and got my shit together, tossing back a swig of beer to settle my stomach.

I BUSTED MY ASS all day running the liquor store. Goddamn hell of a task when you're all by yourself. There was no sign of Joey all day, not even a text. I closed up shop an hour and a half early. I just couldn't hack it anymore. I was exhausted as hell working all day with no breaks. It's just plain inhumane for one person to run a liquor store like this, but we needed the money.

I locked the front door, hopped in my car, and drove home with the windows rolled down. The cool night washed over my sweat-soaked hair. Every few minutes the world started buzzing and everything fell out of focus, then I snapped back to alertness. On my way home, I almost crashed into a stop sign, grazed two parked cars, and barely avoided mowing down some pedestrian. Sleep was all I could think about, like a man in the desert with cold water on his mind. I probably shouldn't have been driving.

Our apartment was still empty when I got home, so I called out, "Joey? You here?"

No reply.

I kicked off my shoes and laid back on the couch. I was so fuckin' zapped, I couldn't think straight, but I knew I needed a bowl and a beer. When was the last time I had a good night's sleep? Must've been several days. Had I ever slept in my life?

I laid out on the couch and stuffed some pillows between my head and the couch arm. It wasn't all that nice, but going with the desert analogy, I felt better dinking camel piss than nothing at all. And for whatever reason, it didn't occur to me that I had a bed in the next room.

Half an hour later, I woke up to the apartment door slamming shut. I jolted upright and instinctively reached for the revolver on my hip. Then I realized I'd been dreaming. I didn't have a gun on my hip, and certainly not an antique single-action cowboy gun like they used in the Old West.

Joey stood in front of the door with balled fists at his sides. He stared at me with hard, unblinking eyes and said nothing. My world spun with a mix of nice buzz and dying headache. For a moment there, I wasn't totally certain about my chances of survival for the next few minutes.

"Where you been, man?" I said.

"Getting you outta trouble," Joey growled. "Pack me a bowl."

He stomped past the living room and riffled through the fridge, then came back with two beers. I dumped the ash out of the bowl and packed some fresh weed.

"Did you talk to the police?"

"Of course," I said. "I called 'em when I found Calvin."

"Fuck."

"What was I supposed to do? Hide his body?" I stuck the bowl in the bong and handed it over. He exchanged it for a freshly opened bottle of IPA.

"Not the worst idea." His voice was almost a monotone.

"You gotta be kidding. What the fuck's the matter with you, man?"

Joey lit the bowl and sucked the smoke through the dirty bong water. Then he leaned back and let a huge smoke cloud rip. He coughed and hacked. "Jesus," he said. "That was rough."

"*Say something*," I shouted.

"Take it easy, you stupid fuckin' asshole. While you've been over here shitting your pants and talkin' to the cops, I went and figured out who did this."

My stomach dropped. "You did?"

"Fuck, yeah. We gotta roll on him right now, though. I heard he's getting ready to dip out."

"I haven't slept in days," I said.

"Then stay here. I'll take care of it."

No, that wouldn't work at all. I jumped off the couch and said, "Fuck it. I'm too wired to sleep. Let's go fuck this guy up."

I was trapped in a nightmare, boxed between a psychopath, a family man, and an honest-to-god mafia. Joey could be a chill guy if you were on his friendly side, but he was also a ruthless fuckin' psychopath. If he got a whiff of you trying to fuck him, he'd fuck you right back. Hell, he'd fuck you *before* you could fuck him. And to my advantage, I was normally too big of a pussy to challenge Joey on anything, and we both knew it. So I had a slim chance of getting out of this alive, so long as I kept letting him believe that.

Joey drove while I sweated in the passenger seat. Right about now, I wished I'd bought myself a gun. I knew Joey kept one on him everywhere he went, but again, it tracks that the world's biggest dumbass wouldn't bother picking one up before something like this happened. I couldn't stop sweating.

"Hey," I said. "You mind if I get a gun after all?"

We stopped at a red light. Joey looked at me and said, "What?"

"I'm kinda nervous. You didn't tell me what we're walkin' into."

Joey thought about that for a second, then he shrugged. "Yeah, I feel you. I wouldn't wanna walk naked into a sitch like this. Check the glove box. I've got a backup in there."

The glovebox swung open, weighed down by a tiny safe that someone had haphazardly bolted into the door of the compartment. The safe was already open, and inside sat a Smith & Wesson revolver with a shortie barrel. I picked it up carefully and checked the cylinder. It was loaded.

"Just make sure you put that back," Joey said. "Or else you owe me two-hundo."

We pulled off the freeway, and my chest pumped with adrenaline. There was only one thing I could think to do, and I was still coming to terms with it. My stomach gurgled, and I thought I might puke. I weighed the revolver in my hands. The grip was moist with sweat. The car swung through a suburban neighborhood and made its way through a cheap apartment complex.

"Where are we going?" I said.

"Right down here."

Joey pulled around the corner and parked in front of a two-story apartment building. The units looked cheap and flat from the outside, freshly painted to cover the fact that they were bargain-bin bullshit for poor people. I shoved the gun in my jeans pocket, and we got out of the car. Joey led me across the lawn and down the way to a plaza with a fountain that didn't run. The last few kids of the evening ran around and played their games. We walked upstairs to the second floor and found a door labeled *25*. This wasn't Andrew's home, but for all I knew, maybe the guy had some girlfriends around town.

"You ready?" Joey said. He took the Kahr K9 pistol out of his jeans and held in front of him, shielded from the kids playing below.

I took a deep breath and pulled the revolver from my pocket. "Yeah."

Joey kicked the door, and it flew to pieces nice and easy. Cheap piece of shit. He ran inside with his pistol aimed forward, and I followed him. My instincts screamed to shoot him in the back and end it right there. But that wouldn't do. We had to find Andrew first.

The living room was empty except for some blanket-covered furniture and a well-vacuumed carpet. Joey hurried back and checked the kitchen, swinging the pistol barrel at each empty corner. Then he came around and gestured at the hallway. If anyone was here, they must've been in the bedroom or the bathroom.

He hung back a second like he expected me to lead the way. But I just stood there, so Joey scoffed and turned down the hallway. He stepped as lightly as possible on the soft rug. There were three doors, and it wasn't clear which one led where. Joey tried the first one and peeked inside. Just a closet. Then the middle door led to a dark bathroom. He flicked the lights on and back off.

We checked the last door. It must've led to a bedroom, but it was locked.

"On me," Joey said. "Keep that fuckin' thing ready, and don't shoot me by accident."

He took me off-guard. I didn't know what to say.

"I'm kidding." He laughed with that kind of uncomfortable chuckle where you're not sure if the joke landed. Before I could figure one way or the other, Joey kicked open the door and disappeared inside, and I ran after him.

"Holy fucking shit," I said.

There was a whole family back here, three young boys and two younger girls. A man and woman shielded them with their bodies, clearly a married couple protecting their kids. But this wasn't Andrew's place — it was Gilbert's.

"What the fuck are you doing, man?" Gil shrieked.

"We're taking back what's ours," Joey said.

Gil's face dropped. He knew right away what we were talking about. Deep down I think I knew what was going on, but I just stood there with a dumbass look on my face and tried to wrap my head around it.

"Hand it over," Joey said. "And we won't hurt you."

One kid started crying, then it rippled out to the rest. The woman crouched and put her arms around them, and Joey instinctively swung his pistol at her. The wife yelped with the anticipation of being shot.

"Stop," I barked. "I'll watch the family. You deal with him."

Gil looked at us with sorrow-twisted brows and said, "I'm sorry, man. We never should've fucked with you like that."

Joey grabbed him by the collar and dragged him out of the bedroom. He belted him across the mouth with the butt of his gun, then dropped him in the hall and said, "Give us our shit, and we'll be off your back."

I held my gun at the family, and my mind whirred. They were really fucking my plan. I couldn't just kill Gil and Joey to shut them up. I'd have to kill his entire family.

"Please," said the woman. "Don't hurt our kids."

"Nobody's gonna hurt you," I said. "If we did, we'd have to kill you all."

That didn't come out the way I meant it. But my brain was fried from a lack of sleep, and I didn't really know what else to do except keep my finger off the trigger until my life was at risk. Right now it wasn't, so I'd stay cool. The kids sobbed, and the woman tried to chill them out. Their welling eyes were fixed on me, and I couldn't stand to look at them.

I swapped the revolver into my other hand and wiped my sweaty palm on my jeans. The barrel shook at the family. I couldn't keep my hands still. Joey came back and threw Gil on the floor in front of his family.

"This is all he's got," Joey said. He showed me a wad of cash and stuck it in his pocket.

"How much?"

"Twenty-five grand." He raised his pistol and fixed the barrel at Gilbert's skull. The woman shrieked and covered her kids' eyes with her arm. "Where's the rest, fuck-o?"

"That's all I've got," Gil sputtered. "I swear to god."

"Who has the rest?"

"The rest of what? We didn't get jack shit from your place. The vault was closed, and the register only had like eighty bucks."

"Well, let's put that in our back pocket," Joey said, "'cause I got no clue what you're talking about. When'd you steal from the register?"

"The stickup," Gil said. He shot his glance at me. "Tris was there. Tell him, man."

"They had masks on," I said. "And they didn't sound like you."

"They were friends of mine."

"Who exactly?" Joey said. "We need names."

"Fuck that. Just shoot me."

"No," begged the woman.

"We're not here to get back at you," Joey said. "We just need the money. Those gook bastards are breaking our fucking balls here."

"Over eighty dollars? You gotta be shitting me."

"Not that night," Joey yelled. "The other night. When you tased me and took the envelope."

"What the fuck are you talking about?"

Joey shoved the Kahr pistol into his waistband and cracked his knuckles. Then he went to work. He delivered a sharp boot across Gil's face and followed it up with a swift kick to the ribs, followed by another kick and another one after that. The kids screamed, and his wife tried to cover their crying faces. Joey kept kicking and kicking.

Dizzy weakness swept over my world. Everything went dark, and I grabbed my knees to stop myself from fainting. I wanted to puke, but nothing came up. When I came to, Joey was still beating on Gil. The man's face was bloody and swollen, and Joey grabbed him by the hair and kept whaling on him until the woman finally let go of her kids and rushed to help her husband.

I cried, "Look out," and aimed the revolver at the woman. It's not like I intended to shoot her. I just wanted her to stand down, but she didn't even react to it. She knocked Joey down and clawed his face while Gil lay gasping on the floor. His hands and legs writhed in dizzied confusion, like he'd been concussed six times over.

Joey covered his face and desperately pushed her away. She kept clawing at his eyes, and he yelped, "Shoot her, for Chrissake!"

The kids screamed. I held the pistol in my shaking hand, but I couldn't squeeze the trigger. Then a thought crossed my mind. What if my bullet missed by just a few inches and hit the wrong target?

Before I could come up with an answer to that question, Joey thrust his forehead into the woman's nose. A loud crack rang out in the room, and she tumbled over and sprawled on the floor. She clutched her bleeding face next to a gasping Gil. Joey stood up panting and blinked the irritation out of his eyes before he gave me his death stare.

"Why didn't you shoot them?" he said.

"Seems like you handled it yourself."

Joey gestured at the door. "Let's go."

8

ME AND JOEY LEFT those kids sobbing over their savagely beaten parents. We didn't exchange a word the whole ride home. When we parked at our apartment, Joey reached past my knees and flicked open the glovebox, where the miniature safe sat empty. I glanced inside, then took the gun out of my pocket and weighed it in my hands.

"How much did you say this was?" I said.

"Why, you wanna keep it?" Joey scoffed. "It was two-hundo."

"How about it's on the store? I'll grab the money from the register tomorrow."

"Whatever, man. Just be careful, it's loaded."

We spent the night drinking, smoking, and watching movies. I managed to squeeze a couple hours of sleep somewhere in between the end of *Die Hard* and the middle of *Predator 2*. When the credits started rolling, I glanced at the window and saw sunlight peeking through the blinds. Morning already. Had I slept at all, or was I just sitting in a trance? I couldn't really say.

JAMES MAXWELL

By eleven in the morning, I felt like a lobotomy patient at work. Joey was alert and well rested, so he drove us and parked in the back lot. Two figures were waiting by the rear door of Calvin's, and the big guy's profile gave them away as Annie and Adrien.

Maybe it was the lack of sleep, but Annie had a funny expression on her face that rubbed me the wrong way. She seemed pleased. Way too pleased for someone who was looking two million dollars. My mind buzzed with the possibilities, and I blinked fast and hard, finding it difficult to stay awake on my feet.

"How's it going?" Annie said. Her expression didn't change. The mountain of a guy had a dead look on his face, like he wasn't all that concerned about what was happening just as long as we kept our hands off Annie.

"Never better," Joey said. "We don't have envelopes, but we could head down to the post office."

"Just give him the cash," Annie said with a nod to her enormous companion. Joey offered the wad of green, and Adrien snatched it away. He counted it and stuffed it in the pocket of his track jacket. Then he leaned toward Annie and whispered something.

"It's all we have for right now," Joey said. "But we've got a lead on the next guy, the asshole with the rest of the stash."

"The rest of what stash?" Annie said.

We gawked at her for a long moment. We were short, and that was the fact of it. $25,000 on a two-million-dollar debt was a hanging offense. Neither of us knew what we could possibly say to save our lives. Annie darted her eyes between us, and she didn't say anything.

"The money," Joey said. "We'll get you more money."

Annie nudged Adrien, who spoke in a low-octave voice like a cartoon caricature of a strongman.

"Turns out you were wrong," he said. "There wasn't nowhere near two million that night. It was only ninety-five K."

"Is that right," I said.

"Yeah," Adrien said. He patted the twenty-five grand in his pocket. "We appreciate your consideration."

76

A big smile grew on Annie's face, the look of a woman who just put her winning hand on the table. "See you boys next week," she said.

They got back in their car and drove off. We stood there and watched them go. Silence passed that felt like ages, and I tried to speak.

"Is that…" I trailed off.

Joey stared beyond the sky and pursed his lips. "Is that what?"

"What I think just happened?"

"Yeah," Joey said. "It was."

I almost passed out when it all washed over me like a black tide. Joey helped me inside, and we took our seats behind the counter. It was half past eleven, and the morning alkies had already come and gone. Some of them had stopped showing up altogether since our schedule was so shaky these days. Joey grabbed a six-pack and opened a beer for each of us, and we drank together.

We didn't talk about it, but we understood the gravity of this situation. We owed seventy grand to the mob, and that meant paying weekly vig to the tune of thousands of dollars for the rest of our lives – or until we could pay off the principal. It made me sick thinking about it. All this bullshit, and for what? I should've seen it coming, but if I had, I wouldn't be the world's biggest dumbass.

We said fuck it. We didn't open shop at all. Instead we spent the day sitting around and drinking the supply to honor the memory of our fallen financial security, Calvin Lenard. But someone showed up around one thirty and ruined our plans when he unlocked the door and stepped inside, nose twitching like a drug-sniffing dog.

"What the fuck?" said the interloper.

We stood up behind the counter. "Who are you?" Joey said.

In retrospect, it should've been clear right away who we were looking at: a jacked Vietnamese American with a red star tattooed on his throat. The guy worked for Annie or her boss, Dennis. That much was obvious on first bluff. He strutted toward the counter with a big grin.

"Smokin' the loud pack, huh?" he said. "Lemme get a hit of that."

"I said who the fuck are you?"

"Relax," said the man. "My dad's Dennis. He sent me to run the place."

"Oh, shit," Joey said. "You're Brandon, right? I haven't seen you in years, bro."

"Yeah, well. We're gonna work together now."

"You're replacing Calvin," I said. My voice was a low monotone, and it came out a lot harsher than I'd intended.

Brandon gave me a look of astonishment and said, "Yeah, pretty much. You got a problem with that?"

"No," I said. "Just making sure we're straight."

He furrowed his brows and scoffed. "Whatever. Listen, you're Joey, right? We gotta talk shop, so let's step back in the office. Buddy boy here can run the counter."

"He's not feeling well," Joey said. "We were just about to close shop for the day."

Brandon blinked and waited for a follow-up or perhaps a punchline. Then he said, "Close shop?"

"That's right."

"Why?"

"Like I said," Joey continued. "He's not feeling well."

"But *you're* feeling fine, right? We can keep the lights on."

"Sure, but I'm grieving. You know?"

"Grieving who? Did your grandma die or something?"

"Who the fuck do you think? Calvin."

"Oh, right. My bad." He blew a puff of air that made his cheeks look like a pufferfish. "Well, shit. I guess that's all right. I didn't really wanna have to work today anyway. Why don't we get started early tomorrow? Let's say ten thirty."

"Sure."

"You go have a good grieving," Brandon said. He reached across the counter and patted Joey's shoulder, then he gave us a fat grin. "Just try to get it out of your system, 'cause I've got enough on my plate between this and the airline restaurant, not to mention my smoke shop up in Oakland. I'm all over the fuckin' place these days, y'know? Anyway, if you can handle all the bullshit for me, that'd be great. I won't be around much. I'll see you guys tomorrow."

Brandon left the liquor store before either of us could say anything. Once he was gone, I laughed dryly. I couldn't think of anything else to do.

"What the fuck's so funny?" Joey said.

"I was just thinking what an asshole he is compared to Calvin."

"Yeah. I was gonna say the same thing."

I STILL HADN'T SLEPT, and my brain was scrambled beyond recognition. Sparks flew across my vision every time I settled my eyes in any direction, and also any time something moved in my periphery. I needed sleep really bad — worse than I'd ever needed to eat or drink or fuck or piss or shit. No wonder sleep torture's so goddamn effective.

Rachel called, and I let it go to voicemail. I was in no mood to talk. I locked my bedroom and smoked a pre-roll joint I'd picked up from the club on my way home. I puffed it once, twice, three times — and I coughed and set it in the ashtray next to my bed. Then I lay down.

Someone pounded on my door. I called out, "What?"

"I'm gonna go get laid," came Joey's muffled voice. "You down?"

"Nah. I gotta get some sleep."

"Pff. Whatever."

The front door slammed shut, and everything was quiet. I sprawled back on my bed and reached for the burning joint in the ashtray. It was just a few inches too far. I leaned over and reached so hard, my arm started to hurt. But the more I stretched, the farther away it seemed to get. Every inch I took just gave it another mile. Was that supposed to be symbolic or something? Because it was just a pile of bullshit. My head thudded on the pillow, and I fell into a deep sleep.

This felt like the first time I'd ever slept in my life. Nourishment like you've never imagined. Like a man come out of the desert eating his first meal in weeks, my brain vomited the overwhelming nourishment of sleep. I was soaked in the nightmares of many futures, my throat deathly dry. I drank from the thermos next to my bed, and I was dry again. Then came more brain vomit.

I dreamt of money, and I dreamt of blood. Blood and money, bloody money, money blood. Money soaked in red syrup that dissolved the paper between your fingers. The more you grasped, the more you lost. My brain's not subtle when it comes to metaphors, and it pissed me the fuck off.

The next day, I woke up at ten thirty feeling hung over. I brushed my teeth and took a shower before work. It was hard to walk straight, and everything in my periphery kept falling out of focus. When I got to the liquor store, which was only ten feet away from my bathroom, Calvin was standing behind the counter, and he grinned at me. Someone had sewn him back together, but they did a really shitty job. He leaked all over the place.

"How's it going?" Calvin said. His voice was a low gurgle. Or maybe he said, "How are you?"

"What are you doing here?" I said. "I thought you were off today."

Calvin got angry and raised his voice, but somehow his words became deeper and more guttural. Harder to understand. "You took the beers from my fridge, Tristian. I know it was you. You broke my heart."

"What do you want me to say?"

Something popped off behind my head, like a gunshot or a firecracker. I whipped around, and then I was standing at a booth in Reed's Indoor Range down in Santa Clara. Joey was in the booth next to me, wearing eye and ear protection and pointing his Kahr K9 downrange. The target was Andrew Chapman, suspended by the armpits with hooks and chains like a hunk of meat. He was pale and dead. Joey shot him the clavicle, then in the heart. No blood came out of his cold body. It was like shooting a frozen pig in a meat hanger.

"You wanna get a few rounds in?" Joey said.

"Nah, I'm good." I took the revolver out of my pocket and weighed it in my hands. Then I checked the cylinder just to be sure. All six rounds were loaded.

"What the fuck are you doing?" Joey said.

"I'm sorry." I swung the cylinder shut and clicked the hammer back. Then I raised the pistol and leveled the barrel at his face. I squeezed my finger like a trigger, but there was nothing in my hand. Like a kid playing guns at recess. I said, *"Bang, bang,"* but it didn't make a difference.

Joey leaned against the counter where his Kahr K9 lay. His hand clutched his chest, and when he let go, a streak of gore came loose in thick coagulated chunks like cheese pulled off a pizza. Blood spilled out of his stomach with the consistency of sewer sludge, piling up on the floor and seeping away slowly. He grabbed his gun off the counter and squeezed the trigger in my face, and a hot burst of fire burned my eyes.

Then I woke up.

The room was dark, with starlight bleeding through the blinds. I was dizzy as hell, and all my senses fuzzied up. It reminded me of my teen years when I was on antidepressants, and I'd forget to take them for a day or two while downing six beers a night. Then I'd wake up feeling exactly like this, dizzy and fuzzy and thirsty as hell, sweating like crazy after a really vivid and fucked-up dream.

I stumbled through the dark apartment and filled a glass of water from the sink in the kitchen. Joey was asleep in his room, or maybe out doing Joey stuff. It was always hard to tell. I glugged down some cold water and filled another glass, then locked myself in my bedroom.

When I did the math in my head, I started to feel okay about everything. Me and Andrew took home $47,500 each. Annie Phan expected weekly vig on that $70,000 "loan." So if we threw down thirty-five K each, we could clear the debt and keep a cool twelve for ourselves. It seemed unlikely Gil would come back around and make a stink of things after the beating we gave him. We could deal with that problem when it cropped up.

I drifted back into a restful sleep.

9

THE NEXT MORNING, I felt like a babe newly born. The world was a colorful place full of light and sound, and I was so happy to be alive. It was half past noon, and I didn't care if the shop was open or if the alkies went home. I was alive, and that was all that mattered.

Around one o'clock, I parked behind Calvin's Liquors and sauntered in through the rear door. Joey stood behind the counter and shrugged at me with a *what-the-fuck* expression. I ignored him and went straight to the bathroom to do my morning business. He was gone when I came back out, and a young man in a waffle-knit shirt and cargo pants stood at the counter with two twelve-packs. Good of him to wait. I rang him up and sold him the beers.

I got off at six in the evening, and Joey came back to take over the liquor store for evening while Brandon smoked blunts in Calvin's old office.

I took off downtown and parked near the old Hotel De Anza. While I didn't hate the place, I didn't like it much either. Too froufrou for my taste. A bunch of pretentious nonsense with inflated prices over some historic landmark bullshit. I parked on the street behind a brand-new bright red Toyota coupe that had no business being left unsupervised in a place like this, a cracked street surrounded by impound lots. I dropped some quarters in the parking meter and bought myself an hour before some meter maid could come by and give me a costly ticket.

A few summer nights back, I'd stayed at Hotel De Anza with an old girlfriend who turned out to be batshit crazy. Walking through this lobby brought back some not-so-nice memories. I went through the lounge, where the light was low and couches and tables were scattered between the bar and a stage with a piano and microphone.

A gorgeous woman in a skimpy silver dress swayed with the microphone and sung cool notes, slurring something unintelligible while a man in a suit danced his fingers on the keys. It was all so goddamn predictable, wasn't it? Like if you typed *nightclub* into an AI image generator.

I saw Andrew sitting alone at the bar, and I walked over and ordered a double IPA. The bartender served me up and went back to the opposite corner to lean against the counter and watch that beautiful woman sing her quiet heart out.

"How's it going?" I said in a hushed tone.

"Fine. And you?"

"Just great. I finally got some sleep last night. Look, we've got a problem, though."

The singer swooned into her final note, and the pianist erupted into a crescendo. And just like that, it was over. Dead silence. A few moments passed before the drunk rich folk sprawled out on the couches started clapping half-heartedly, and the piano warmed up for the next song while the singer kept swaying.

"You mean besides the bastards hunting me?" Andrew growled.

"Well, no, that's pretty much it. Listen, we gotta give the money back."

The piano riff settled into a cool rhythm, and the woman started singing some familiar lyrics: *There's a long goodbye...*

"What do you mean?" Andrew said. "I can't do that."

"Not all of it. Just seventy thou in total. I did the math: if we each put down thirty-five K, we'd pay off the principle and take home twelve-point-five each. No sweat, no trouble with the Viet mob."

"Yeah. That's not gonna happen."

A man in the audience loved this song. He stood up and started clapping and singing poorly along. But instead of lyrics, he babbled nonsense like a three-year-old. *There's a lawn hood lie…*

"Why not?"

"I spent most of it," Andrew said.

"Lemme guess. You bought a bright red Toyota coupe."

Andrew grinned and said, "You saw it? Nice, huh."

"How much?" I sneered.

"Well, it was just south of thirty-five K brand new. But I looked around on Craigslist and saw one as cheap as twenty-four."

"So how much did you spend?"

"I bought it new," Andrew said. "Thirty-five."

"Jesus fucking Christ. You've gotta be shitting me."

Goodbye, goodbye, goodbye, goodbye, she sang.

"I know, right?" Andrew said. "And the resale value drops like a rock the moment you drive it off the lot. It's fuckin' bullshit."

I swigged back the beer and steadied myself on the counter, but I felt dizzy as hell. It took everything in me to stop from blacking out.

At this point, I might be better off blasting this guy, pawning the fucking car, and scrounging up everything I could to pay Annie her $70,000. But there might be a way out of this without stooping to murder. So I stowed that thought, but it was always there in the back of my mind. Like watching the exit sign at a shitty show that's not quite boring enough to leave.

"Anyway," Andrew said, "I wouldn't give up the money even if I had it."

"I need what you've got left. The twelve K or whatever. I'll put all my money in, and then we'll just need ten for the principal."

"What'd I just say?"

"Motherfucker, this is our skin here. You're really gonna skimp out on me?"

"You said you had it under control," Andrew whined. "What happened to your fall guy?"

"It didn't work out," I said. "He only had twenty-five on him. That's why we only have to pay seventy. But Joey said he's coming up with some names, some more guys from that crew who might have money."

"So you're gonna rob more people."

I laughed humorlessly, but Andrew just stared me down and didn't react. "Well, sure," I said. "But they're scumbags. They're not real people. Right?"

"Sure," Andrew said. "Just a bunch of scumbags."

That's when it occurred to me that Detective King had approached him at some point to make the same offer she made me. There was a non-zero chance that he took her up on it. And if he did, I was fucked already, talking all this incriminating shit. I chose my next words very carefully.

"See you around."

Part Four — All In

10

THE NEXT DAY, Andrew came by the store around eleven in the morning, just after opening time, and bought his usual twelve-pack of Sierra Nevada. Joey didn't start until four, and Brandon was tucked away in his hole behind that door marked *PRIVATE*. Andrew and I exchanged no words. Like we didn't even know each other. In retrospect, that might've been cause for suspicion, but Brandon was too new to realize Andrew was a chummy regular. Not that the stupid son of a bitch was paying any attention anyways.

Four o'clock came and went, and Joey never showed up for his shift. I called him on his cell, and it went straight to voice mail. His phone was turned off or dead. Maybe *he* was dead. That would be real inconvenient to this whole debt situation. I packed a bowl in the glass pipe and smoked it, then I kicked up my feet and crossed them on the counter next to the register. Brandon seemed like a real asshole, but to his credit he didn't have anything resembling a work ethic, so he didn't give a shit about us smoking weed in the shop or taking beers.

It took a while to settle in — or incubate or whatever — but it really pissed me off when I thought about Rachel. She must've had something to do with all this, one way or another. After all, I'd spilled my purse all over her floor like a fucking idiot. She was probably in cahoots with Gilbert or Andrew — or maybe even Detective King. Hell, why not all three? You could never tell with someone like her, sleeping with a guy and not telling him she was already taken by a woman.

Joey bailed on his shift, so I manned the shop for the rest of the evening, smoking enough bowls to keep my rage alleviated until I could properly express it to his face. Around 9:45, I was exhausted and had nothing left in me. I knocked on the door marked **PRIVATE** and called out to Brandon.

"Hey, man. I've been here since we opened. You mind if I take off?"

No reply. I knocked louder and tried the doorknob. It was unlocked. The room was dark and empty. He'd never even been here in the first place.

I closed the store and drove back to my apartment, wanting nothing more than to throw myself on the couch and watch a movie on TV. When I reached our door, I heard them inside.

Joey was on the couch with one of his regular call girls — Jenny or some such — and they were sharing a joint and a six-pack while they watched the Maury show. When I walked in, Joey said something incomprehensible over his bloated, red-faced laughter. I ignored them and went back to my room, turning on the standing fan loud enough to drown them out.

I was scheduled to open Calvin's again the next morning, and I woke up feeling foggy as hell and half-asleep. The living room was littered with beer cans and discarded slices of pizza. Must've been some kind of drunken food fight. Joey's door was closed, quiet, and presumably locked. There was no way I'd hang around and deal with any of it. For once, I was glad to go to work.

My relief washed away when I saw the state of Calvin's Liquors. The windows were smashed apart, and someone had ransacked and destroyed the stock. When I entered the store, Annie and Adrien emerged from the aisles, and Joey rose from behind the counter.

"What the hell happened?" I said.

"You tell me," Joey said. "Your friends did it."

"Who, Gil? He's not my fuckin' friend."

"Not him," Annie corrected. "His crew. They broke into the manager's office and took the hard drive."

"Yeah," Joey said. "But a cop drove by. He saw it go down, and he told us everything."

"So who did this, exactly?"

"Those weasels who held you up," she said. "Marty Franco and Nico Muñoz."

"Fuck. Where's Gil?"

"He's still in the hospital," she said. "Which is where your ass is gonna go if you don't help us find these assholes."

That was all the convincing I needed. It wasn't like I had some private knowledge about Gilbert's amigos. I was just clueless as the rest of them. For all I knew, they all could've been churchmates.

We took 280 South to 101 and got off on Capitol Expressway. According to Annie's sources — undoubtedly some crooked cop working for the SJPD — the targets had been hiding out at an apartment leased to someone named Oscar Correa and his girlfriend, Andrea Cortés. That meant at least four people — guaranteed collateral damage.

I didn't like the sound of any of this, but I didn't say shit. Joey was in the back seat next to me, watching morning traffic through the passenger window like a sad dog on his way to the vet. We cruised across the city to East Side San Jose, then through a neighborhood made of hand-me-down suburban homes and cheap apartment housing. Adrien pulled the car into a cul-de-sac and parked in front of a three-story complex, pointing the car back down toward the road.

Annie leaned over the headrest from the passenger seat and said, "Ready?"

I poured sweat in the backseat, palm slick on the handle of my snub-nose revolver. It felt awkward as hell in my hands. Joey nodded, took the Kahr K9 out of his waistband, and racked the slide.

"Let's go," Annie said.

They said the apartment was labeled 1A, meaning unit A, level 1. But the units weren't lettered, they were just numbered, and the labels said 101, 102, 103, and so on. We gawked in the courtyard like a bunch of morons, swinging our heads around and covering our guns with our shirts.

"What'd you say the room was?" Adrien said. His shotgun wouldn't quite fit in his custom-fit shirt, so he'd stuck it in his pants leg and staggered around like someone with a stiff leg from a war wound.

"Goddamnit," Annie growled. She stuck her pistol into the pocket of her skinny jeans with the handle and trigger sticking out, then she took her phone and looked through her messages.

"What the fuck are we doing here, Annie?" he said. Me and Joey stayed quiet, waiting our turn and holding on to the urge to run the fuck away.

"Hold up," she said. Then she chuckled. "My bad. I was looking at next week."

Adrien kicked open the front door of apartment 108. The inside was dark except for the blue glow of a television set, and he stormed in with the shotgun forward and a barrel-mounted flashlight leading his way. The man was shockingly nimble for his size. Annie followed him, then came me and Joey. I flicked the light switch, and the room lit up. Someone had left the TV running on an old black-and-white film where Humphrey Bogart was flirting with Lauren Bacall.

Adrien swung through the next doorway and entered a long, narrow hall. It was dark and empty, and there were doors everywhere. Three closed on the right, and a kitchen doorway on the left with swinging saloon-style panels. The light was on inside, and somebody was in there — several somebodies muttering to each other.

He swung around the corner and aimed the shotgun into the kitchen. Two people stood there, a man and a woman. The man had his pistol fixed at the doorway, but he was too late figuring things out. The shotgun's flashlight might've given him the impression they were cops.

The man held his fire, and that was a big mistake. Adrien blew him away with the deafening punch of buckshot. His chest tore open, and you could see the light coming through the other side of him. He dropped like a bag of shit, and his pistol clattered at the woman's feet.

Adrien swung the shotgun at her and pumped a smoking shell onto the tile floor. She put up her palms and cried out, "Don't shoot me! I'm pregnant."

He hesitated, then lowered his gun. In that same instant, the woman reached for the small of her back and whipped her hand forward. Another blast rang out in the tiny room, and Adrien fell limp on the floor. Trickles of blood splattered my face and Annie's. My ears yammered in that way where you'll never hear right again. The woman pointed her tiny black pistol at us, but with Adrien out of the fight, she didn't quite know who to shoot next.

That split-second delay gave Annie a chance to crouch down and aim into the kitchen, then she pulled her trigger. And she pulled it again and again and again and again. A whole mag of bullets perforated the woman until the gun clicked on empty. The woman staggered against the kitchen counter and coughed up blood, like she was trying to say something. Then she hit the tile floor with a splat.

"Jesus Christ," I yelled. "Who the fuck are these people? Is this even the right place?"

Annie didn't seemed fazed by any of this. She kneeled down and peeled the shotgun out of the dead fat man's hands, then she twisted around and shoved the gun into my chest.

"Go on," she said, "or I'll skin you alive."

Right about now, an obvious thought crossed my mind. Why not blast her head off with this shotgun right now? Or better yet, grab a bad guy's gun and pump a round into the base of her skull. She stared me down with a grimace, like she was privy to my plans, and she grabbed my collar and shoved me ahead into the hallway.

"You go first." She pointed her pistol at Joey. "And you back him up."

"All right." My voice wavered.

I cleared the three bedrooms from right to left. The first room was unlocked, and I swung open the door and pointed the under-mounted flashlight inside. It looked like a child's room. I stood there, trembling. Nothing could compel me to go inside.

"Go on," Annie said.

I stepped clumsily into the room and waved the shotgun around, checking each corner twice. I couldn't see anyone. Joey came in after me and flicked the light switch, and I flinched at the shock of the lamp turning on.

"It's empty, you fuckin' moron," he said.

The next room was locked. Judging by the space between doors, it was the smallest of the three rooms. Probably a bathroom. I could feel Annie's hostile stare on the back of my neck, so I took a step back and gave the door my best kick.

Pain cracked in my ankle, and I fell back against the wall and slid to the floor.

"Aw, fuck," I shrieked. "My leg!"

"You're a goddamn idiot," Joey said. He ripped the shotgun out of my hands and gave the door a swift kick that bucked it right open. Then, in a single swift motion, he swung inside and flicked on the light switch.

I got up on my feet, my ankle burning under my weight. This room was a bathroom, all right, and a naked man was sitting on the tile floor. His clothes were piled up in the bathtub next to him, and he had headphones covering his ears, the big sound-canceling kind like you'd use in a studio. He didn't seem to be aware there were intruders in the bathroom.

"That's him," Annie said. "Nico Muñoz."

"Are you shitting me?" Joey said. "He's skagged out."

Joey tore the headset off Nico's ears, and the man glanced up at us with a sweat-gleaming brow. He opened his mouth and yelped.

"Jesus Christ," Joey moaned.

Nico moved his mouth like he was chewing or talking, but no sound came out.

"Go check the next room," Annie said. "I'll take care of him."

I fully expected this man to be dead the minute we walked away. But what the hell. It wasn't my job to save someone's life. Annie kneeled down in the bathroom and started whispering to the man, asking him questions that seemed to pique his interest.

Me and Joey approached the last door and tried the knob, but it was locked. "Well," I said. "You're gonna have to get this one. My ankle's fucked up."

Joey kicked the door and sent it swinging off its hinges, then he stormed the room with the shotgun aimed forward. I braced myself for that room-shaking, teeth-chattering blast of a twelve-gauge. But there was just silence.

"Hey Tris," came his voice from the room. "Tell Annie not to kill that guy."

I peered back into the bathroom, where Annie kneeled down, whispering to Nico. "I think she's got it under control," I said. "Why, what's wrong?"

The stench inside the master bedroom was horrible. I covered my face and hobbled inside. Joey stood between the bed and a laptop on a dresser that showed the Netflix logo and a prompt that asked if you're still watching. On the bed lay the pale remains of a man who'd clearly died of an overdose several days before. He was locked in a leisurely posture with a syringe hooked to his emaciated arm. I gagged when I tried to speak.

"Is this the other guy?"

Joey kneeled down and rooted around under the bed. He pulled out a black duffel bag and zipped it open. There were a pair of pistols inside. Joey stood up and showed me the contents of the bag.

"These the gats they stuck in your face?"

"I guess," I said. "I didn't pay attention."

"Well, shit. At least we got one of 'em."

NICO WAS THE SMALLER of the two robbers, so it was no problem taking him outside and stuffing him in the back of the car. His bud Marty must've overdosed treating his ankle, or maybe he just got scared and folded. It didn't matter much either way. We drove down to South San Jose and went into a neighborhood where every other house was overgrown and abandoned. There were three vacants at the end of a cul-de-sac, and we pulled into the driveway of the middle one.

The house was peeled away and its windows were shuttered. This place was nice and tucked away back here in this cutty little cul-de-sac, and it wasn't clear if anyone was staying in the other houses. The vacant next door had its door busted open, and there was candlelight upstairs and a slow stream of smoke pouring out like from weed or a hookah. Across the cul-de-sac there were two houses that had trimmed lawns and all their windows intact. The paint jobs didn't look much better, but you could tell a mile away that somebody legit was living there. We didn't see anyone when we pulled in.

Annie got out of the driver's seat and swung open the garage door. She gestured to Joey, and he climbed over the center console and sat down behind the wheel. He pulled the car into the garage, and Annie shut us into darkness.

I panicked for a moment in the blackness, thinking that was it — the trap sprung. I reached for my gun, but some part of me told me it was too late, and I'd have more dignity if I didn't yank it at them. In retrospect, that didn't make any sense at all, but I'm glad that urge kicked in because it saved my life.

The light in the garage flickered on, and Annie yanked open the car door and pulled our drugged-out captive onto the cement floor. I sat there trembling with my hand buried in my pocket.

Annie looked at me and said, "What?"

I don't think I could've gotten out of that car and into that house any faster unless I sprinted. She watched me go inside, and I didn't want to know what she was thinking right then.

The interior was completely trashed. The front door was intact and even had a lock, but the rear sliding door had been smashed ages ago. Years of outlaws and vagrants and runaways had come here for a night or two, and more than a few of them had thrown parties that apparently involved alcohol and violence. Dirt had been tracked all over the inside, and the corners were adorned with puddles of bodily fluid. I saw an old brown blood stain on one wall, plus a pool of vomit in the kitchen. There was nowhere to sit or stand that wasn't covered in filth, like some terrible mud-storm had raged through.

I brushed the dirt off a chair, sat down at the kitchen table, and lit up a cigarette. Joey and Annie carried our prisoner downstairs to the basement, and I sat around blowing clouds of smoke. The counters were covered in rotten fruit, and the place smelled awful. I'm not sure if the smoke covered up the stench, or if it just blasted out my sense of smell with tobacco, but either way, it did the job.

Annie didn't seem bothered by Adrien's death. She made a discreet call to papa Dennis to let him know what happened, requesting backup like she was asking Dad for allowance. That probably meant a couple more beefy Viet guys. It could be good news, but it was more likely bad.

We spent the day at the safehouse. A few hours and a couple calls to the SJPD later, we got the rundown from a flatfoot who must've banked hundreds of thousands a year on Dennis Phan's dime. He confirmed the death toll at the apartment: Martin Franco was in the morgue along with Adrien Nguyen, Oscar Correa, and Andrea Cortés. There was no official reason for Nico Muñoz to have been there, so nobody had filed a missing report on him.

That was good news for us, but not so good for Nico, who was a little tied up at the moment. Get it? Tied up. We strung him to a shit-stained toilet in the basement that'd never been ripped out after renovations ended six months ago, around the time the previous owner bust out and lost everything to Annie Phan. The smell in the basement was enough to make you puke if you didn't have a steel stomach.

The kitchen didn't smell half as bad as the basement. Joey swung open the old refrigerator and gagged, then slammed it shut.

"Don't open that," Annie said. "It's all rotten."

"Yeah, no shit," he said. "We gotta get some baking soda in there."

Right about now I really wished I had a beer or a joint in my hands. My bones shook from the trauma of seeing those people get blown away. The words *Don't shoot, I'm pregnant*, rang in my head like an echoing gunshot. I asked about it a few times, and each time Joey explained that it was just a ruse to get Adrien to let his guard down — and it had worked. I kept forgetting and asking again until Annie got pissed and told me to shut the fuck up.

Then I shut my mouth.

"So how's our amigo?" she said.

"Semiconscious," Joey said. "It'll take be a while before he wakes up. Then we'll dangle a couple hits in front of him like a carrot on a stick." He chuckled. "If he doesn't wanna die from dope shock, he'll have to tell us what we want."

"I've got some better ideas," Annie said. "You let me call the shots."

"I'm gonna step out for a smoke," I said.

"No," Annie replied harshly. "It'll draw attention. Just open a window."

I went over to the kitchen window and tried to yank it open, but it was stuck from years of atrophy. There was a sliding glass door that led outside, so I unlocked that and slid it open. Then I lit up.

It didn't take long for Joey and Annie to do the same thing. We were gonna wait a while, after all. Might as well have fun with it. I offered to pick us up some beers, but Joey shot me down. He said he'd go do it himself.

I waited in that filthy kitchen with Annie, the dim light of the lamp casting a gray shadow over her features. She watched me relentlessly. More than was socially acceptable, I figured, so something must've been going on.

But I didn't say anything. I knew what she was doing. If I said something, it'd make me look worse.

Joey returned an hour later, not just with beers but with an ounce of weed. I can't tell you any other time I went faster from pissed off to relieved as hell. We rolled joints and blunts and packed bowls and cracked beers. The sun went down, and we kept smoking and drinking deep into the night. Just before eleven, Joey went downstairs to check on our friend. He came back up with a smirk.

"He's awake."

Annie stood up, stubbed out her cigarette on the table, and walked down the stairs. Joey stood at the doorway, waiting for me. The smell from the basement wafted out, and I covered my mouth.

"Come on," he said.

I stepped down into the filthy basement, where our prisoner was tied to a chair with wet rope that looked like it'd been rotting in rainwater for the better part of a year. Nico Muñoz was naked and knotted in ligatures. His bronze skin glistened in the basement light, slick with a layer of sweat while he dreamed sweet coma dreams.

"I thought he woke up," I said.

"Well, he fell back asleep," Joey grunted.

"I've got an idea," Annie said.

She quarterbacked Joey while he carried out the dirty work. He had a whole toolbox to work with: pliers and hammers and screwdrivers and even some blades. Annie instructed him to be gentle — but not too gentle — when he woke our guest up. They started with the pliers, and within seconds he began to scream so loud that it never stopped ringing in my ears.

That's when I looked around and realized the basement was soundproofed. He wasn't the first captive to be brought here, and he wouldn't be the last.

Nico struggled against his restraints like a wild animal caught in a trap. When he tired himself out, he sat there panting and drooling, switching his gaze between the three of us.

"I know you," he said to me between heavy breaths. "But who the fuck are you guys?"

"My name's Chuck," Joey said, "and you're shit outta luck."

"Fuck you," snarled the captive.

"Give it to him again," Annie said.

Joey held a box cutter in front of Nico. The man stared at him unflinching with bloodshot eyes. Joey waited, as if the man might answer a question they hadn't asked. Then he pushed open the blade, bent down to the prisoner's fingers, and got to work.

The man screamed and screamed.

I couldn't take it. I stomped up the stairs, ran out back through the paneless sliding door, and puked on the dead grass. My world was spinning, and I thought I could still hear the man screaming. But Joey had closed the door behind me. It was just echoing in my thoughts. I can still hear him sometimes.

Once I spat the last bit of yuck out of my mouth, I lit a fresh cigarette and stood there in the desolate yard, watching the sky. It was chilly in the late night, and stars swarmed across the sky. I blew a puff of smoke, and it dissipated into the heavens.

I gathered my nerves and went back downstairs. It was the stink of it all more than anything, thinking back. I sometimes smell that stench in my dreams. When I went downstairs, Nico was sobbing between breaths. Joey leaned back against the wall with his bloody pliers, and Annie waited on the other side of the victim with her arms crossed. They were waiting for him to stop mewling so he could talk.

"Jesus Christ," I groaned. But my voice didn't carry over the noise.

"Okay," Nico blubbered. "I'll talk. I'll talk."

"About what?" Annie said.

"Whatever you wanna know."

"Such as?"

"*Fuck you*," he screamed. "I don't know what the fuck you wanna know."

She nodded at Joey, and he approached the man with the pliers ready.

"Wait-wait-wait-wait-wait," he belted out like a machine gun. "You wanna know about Gilbert and his whole scam. Right?"

Annie raised her hand, and Joey backed off. "Maybe," she said. "What do you wanna know?"

She shot a glance back at her personal torturer.

"*Wait*," Nico shrieked. "Okay, okay. Gil runs the crew, me and Marty just work for him. He told us he was gonna drum up some business at Calvin's Liquors, get a little squeeze going, but the guy didn't play ball. So then he had us knock the place over."

"And that was you and Marty who did that," Joey said.

"That's right. We didn't get jack shit out of it, either. This fucking guy here," he nodded at me, "was working that night, and he fuckin' bluffed us out."

I couldn't help but smirk. "Yeah, I did."

"Shut up," Joey snapped at me. Then he turned his attention back to the prisoner. "So you got jack shit. Then what?"

"Gil told us to lie low," he said. "So I cashed out some assets and stocked up on necessities."

"And that's when we found you," Annie said.

"Yeah. I guess you found Marty too, right?"

"Sure," Joey said. "Whatever's left of him."

"What happened to Oscar and Andrea?"

"They're dead," Annie said. "And they killed my associate. He was worth about four of you pathetic little bitches, so I'd say we're even."

Nico scoffed and said nothing.

"So when did all this leave you time to tase me for my fuckin' envelope?" Joey said.

There's a certain clarity in that moment when a torture victim's giving up the goods, and then you throw him a genuine curveball. Nico looked at him like he was speaking Martian.

"Your what?" Nico said.

"Go ahead," Annie grunted.

"*Wait*," Nico shrieked. "I don't know what you're talking about. We've been hiding out after the robbery. If someone knocked you down a second time, it wasn't us. I swear to God."

"Could it have been Gil?" she said.

"I doubt it. Last I heard, he's in the hospital."

Annie and Joey exchanged looks and shot a glare at me. I blinked. I couldn't help it — they saw right through me. But neither of them said anything. They turned their attention back to the prisoner.

"Do you know anyone else who was scoping the place out?" Annie said.

"Which place?"

"Either one. The liquor store or the coffee shop."

The tortured man panted and bled. His eyes darted between the three of us, and for a moment it didn't seem like he had an answer. Annie raised her hand to wave Joey back to work, but before she could complete the motion, Nico started talking.

"There was this other guy," he said. "Last October, I think. He came to us about your liquor store, said some nights you get money from the VIP game stashed in that safe."

I started to sweat. There was no way this could end well for me.

"Okay," Annie said. "So then what?"

"Then nothing," Nico said. "It died on the vine. Guy seemed sketchy as hell. He was all caught up in some bullshit, so we never went through with it."

"What was his name?"

"Andrew something," he said. "I guess he went to school with Gil."

My natural instinct was to panic, but I managed to keep my cool. Annie and Joey exchanged glances, then they looked at me.

"Andrew," Joey said. "Isn't that the name of the guy who comes into our shop?"

"It is," I confirmed.

"Fuckin' bastard," he barked. "Was that the asshole who tased me? I'll kill him."

"What's his last name?" Annie said.

Joey shrugged, and they looked at me again.

"I'm not sure," I said. "Maybe we could check his receipts."

"Fuck me," Joey said with an excited clap. "You're a genius, man. Let's go back to the shop."

"Hold on." Annie's voice was a booming authority. "I'm going with you. Tristian stays here to watch this asshole."

Joey shrugged and said, "Fine by me. You got a problem with that, Tris?"

"Of course not."

I followed them upstairs and sparked a new cigarette while they piled into the car and took off down the street. I watched them through a loose board in the living room window, and once their car was gone, I stubbed the cigarette and went back down to the basement.

Nico was smiling when I came off the steps. He looked like he'd been waiting for this moment.

"You're Tristian Sloan," he said, hoarse from all the screaming. "Right?"

"That's right," I said.

He chuckled and let out a heavy breath. His naked body gleamed with sweat and blood. I tried my best to focus on his eyes and look away from his wounds.

"You know what you could do," he said. "You could cut me loose right now, and it'd be good for you."

"I could, huh?"

"Yeah. You drive me to a hospital — or, shit, just set me loose, I'll get myself there — and next time I see Gilbert, we'll take care of all these problems you've got."

"You can do that, can't you?"

His confidence faltered. He took heavy breaths and spat blood on the floor. "Look, we can help each other here. You, me, and Gil. We'll take out these gook fucks and hand you over that fuckin' friend of yours. You can do whatever you like with him."

"I guess I can."

"What the fuck do you want?" he snapped. "An apology? I'm sorry we fuckin' robbed you. But I can help you find Andrew. I just need you to set me free."

"Where is he?"

"Well, off the top of my head, I don't know. But I could—"

I raised my pistol out of my pocket and leveled the barrel at Nico's chest. Then I hesitated, and the man stopped talking. He just stared unblinking like we were frozen in time together. Hours passed by in that split-second before I pulled the trigger.

I shot him three times in the chest, and the blasts in that sound-proof room blew out my ears. He sat there squirming with blood pumping out of those gaping wounds, life leaking out of him, and as the seconds passed he got stiller and the world got quieter. The ringing faded out of my ears, and I was left there with the stench of gunpowder in my nose. Nico was nothing more than a chunk of bloody raw meat now.

I pocketed the revolver and left the house. It wasn't exactly master criminal planning on my part. I was outside before I realized I'd been left without a ride, so I got on my phone and called up an Uber to pick me up. I wandered out of the neighborhood, and my sweat cooled in the night air. I must've been walking for twenty minutes before my ride picked me up, and at any point during that time someone could've rolled on me.

11

MY UBER DROPPED ME OFF at my car, and I drove it back to Andrew Chapman's house and parked around the block. When I walked around and reached his residence, the last person in the world I wanted to see was making her way back from the front door. Detective King crossed the front lawn and spotted me before I could duck back and hide.

"Mister Sloan," she said. "Glad I ran into you."

"Call me Tris."

We shook hands, and she gave me a grimace that let me know right off the bat there was no good news.

"I understand you're friends with Mister Chapman," she said.

I felt like my heart would implode in my chest. I couldn't take much more of this shit. I barely squeaked out the words, "What happened?"

"He's vanished. Took off with his family and a newly bought coupe, and he put his house on the market. Nobody's been able to get in touch with him."

"Really?"

She shrugged. "Yeah, it happened this morning, most likely. Hell, I'm surprised he stayed as long as he did."

"What do you mean?"

"You know. Just given his record and all."

I was sweating, but I'd never felt colder in my life. I said, "What record?"

"Just your garden-variety gang stuff," she said. "He got pinched smuggling a pound of heroin from Mexico to California. Gave up his associates and served, oh, I don't know. Was it five months, or six?"

I could barely speak. My voice came a mumble. "He did time?"

"Yeah, county jail. They let him out on good behavior." She stared at me and waited for a reply.

"Okay. Thanks, I guess."

"For what?"

"I don't know. Why are you telling me this?"

"You asked." She chuckled. "Look. Since we're on the topic, I'd like to make a deal with you, Tristian."

"What the hell are you talking about?"

"Maybe it's better if we go back to the station," she said. "Talk it over somewhere safe."

"I'm not gonna fuckin' rat, if that's what you're saying."

"Seems it did your friend plenty of favors."

"They'd kill me." I couldn't believe my big fucking mouth. I shut it and glanced around to make sure nobody was in earshot, then I growled, "Leave me the fuck alone."

I turned back to my car, and she tailed after me, saying in a hushed tone, "We'll protect you from reprisal. I can get you off any crimes you committed, so long as they're not murder or something federal."

I told her to fuck off, and I fired up my engine and got outta there quick. As soon as I was out of her sight, I pulled over to the side of the road, opened the door, and puked my guts into the street. Numbness overwhelmed my body, and I felt sick and dizzy. I slammed the door and kept driving. The last thing I needed was King or some other cop rolling up on me and asking what was wrong.

Acid jolted up from my stomach and burned my throat with the fervor of wretched sickness. I headed back to our apartment with no fuckin' idea what to do next, and when I stopped at a red light, I finally got the chance to think things over for a second.

And I started sobbing. I'd never killed anyone in my life. Why did I kill Nico Muñoz? Annie and Joey left the place talking about receipts and tracking Andrew down, and I just fuckin' panicked. Then he admitted he didn't even know where Andrew was, so I plugged him. I gagged thinking about it. The man was slain by my own hand. If that black mark on my soul wasn't enough, it was only a matter of time before Joey and Annie returned to the hideout and found what I'd done.

I had to find Andrew before either of them. If they got their hands on him, it was all over. He'd say my name, and I would have to die. That was the compromise I made when I pulled him into this scheme. It was all in the name of the money: two million dollars split evenly two ways. I didn't regret my choice, but if I could do it over again, I obviously wouldn't have bothered.

But I had no choice but to fold or keep calling. So I called.

When I got back home, I cleared the apartment with my revolver just in case Annie and Joey had some friends waiting to surprise me. The place was empty. I cracked a beer and smoked a bowl, my hands trembling violently. It was about the only thing that could keep me calm.

I'd seen Andrew a lot back in high school, and we stayed in touch even though we stopped kicking it. After all, my store was close to the house he'd inherited from his parents, so he dropped by on the regular. The only other family he had in the area was an older brother, and the man was a bit of a loser. He never held down a job, and he lived off welfare checks in his guest bedroom. He was kind of a hanger-on once Andrew got married and had a son.

So that was three potential threats: Andrew, his wife, and his brother. What were their names? Shit, I didn't remember. But the son was like, eight years old at the time, so I didn't have to worry about him pulling a gun and popping me.

The only lead I had on this fucking guy was the coupe he'd bought. I saw it outside the Hotel De Anza the last time I saw him. I didn't bother looking at the plate, but I figured if I glanced around on Craigslist, something might come up.

Lo and behold! A listing created this morning for a red coupe, almost brand new, with 25% knocked off the asking price. In other words, someone who needed to offload the thing right now.

I finished my beer and stuck my pistol back in my pocket. Before I headed out, I went back to my bedroom and fetched the envelope from under my bed. It held my half of the take — all forty-seven-point-five. I stuffed the envelope into my pocket and got moving.

Naturally, the coupe's seller refused to accept any text or email exchange. They wanted a phone call to vet the buyer before meeting up to make the sale. But Andrew wasn't as clever as he thought he was. I downloaded a voice modulator app on my phone, pitched it up, and did my girl voice when I called him up. He didn't recognize me, as far as I could tell. I offered twenty-five grand in cash for the coupe, and he sounded delighted.

He gave me the name of the hotel where he was staying, a shitty little place by the San Jose airport. I grinned and thanked him, then I hung up. I chugged down the rest of my beer and headed out.

I pulled into the parking lot of the motel and cut off my car's headlights. Everything submerged into darkness around me. I closed my eyes, and for a few moments it was just like I was dead. It was calm and peaceful, like none of this even mattered. And I knew that's what I'd really wanted all along. I just wanted to die.

The winter chill seeped into my bones, and I shivered in the driver seat of my car. I turned on the voice modulator app and called Andrew. He picked up on the first ring.

"Hello?"

I talked in my girl voice. "Hey, it's Lizzy. I'm at the motel, but I don't see the coupe."

"It's in the rear lot. I'll come out and meet you. Where are you?"

"I just got here. I think I'm by the front office."

"All right," he said. "I'll be right there."

I put my phone in my pocket and took out my gun. Then I sat in the dark and waited. The night was cold and my fingers were numb. I breathed heat into my hands and scanned the lot. No sign of him yet.

Then a door opened: first floor, labeled 15A. Andrew stuck his head out and glanced around discreetly, showing himself for no more than two seconds. Then he was gone.

He called me back on my burner number and said, "Hey, where are you?"

"I think I just saw you," I said in my girly voice. "Was that you up in 26B?"

"No," he said. "Hang on, I'll come out. Park somewhere and step outside so I can see you."

I didn't bother hanging up. I dropped the phone on the center console and hopped out of the driver's seat of my car, then led the way with my revolver aimed forward. I ran over to room 15A and slowed down just when the door came ajar and Andrew peered out again.

If I were a second later, I'd have been a dead man. I pressed myself against the wall next to the neighboring door, and Andrew stuck the double barrels of a shotgun out into the cool air of the night and scanned the area. I held my pistol forward and slid against the wall, inching closer to Andrew's door. This was my chance, and if I fucked it up, I knew I wouldn't get another one.

The door slammed shut just as I was gonna lunge at him. I let out a stale breath and held my gun in a shaking hand. *Son of a bitch*, I thought. *If I'd just been a few seconds quicker...*

Then I heard the click and slide of dragging metal on the other side of the door. Andrew yanked the deadbolt loose and flung the door open, then he stepped outside and looked around. I ran at him and grabbed him by the shirt, then I shoved him back into the room and slammed the door shut behind me.

Andrew lay on the carpet in front of me with his palms up. The shotgun had come loose from his grip and lay in the middle of the living room, right between the couch, the television, and the little kitchen area.

A woman and a young child cowered on the couch — Andrew's wife and son, I guessed. I spotted another man in the bathroom right before the door slammed shut.

I stood with my back against the door and leveled my pistol down at Andrew's chest. His lips trembled, and he tried to say something. I didn't really wanna hear him speak, but I didn't know if I had it in me to shoot him. I hesitated. And he took that as an invitation to talk his way out of this mess, which really pissed me off.

"Hold up now," Andrew said. "We can still work this out."

There was no way he could make a move without me knowing it. I clicked back the hammer of my revolver.

"How's that?" I said. "You already fucked me."

"Let's take this somewhere private, huh?" Andrew said. He started to push himself upright, but I shoved my gun at him, and he thought better of that. "I don't talk business in front of my family."

"It's not business," I said.

"Wait a minute," he said. "Look, I don't expect you to—"

I plugged him twice in the chest, and he lay there blinking in shock. Then I raised my pistol and squeezed the last round into his forehead. Blood and brain matter spattered on the wall and his wife and kid. Andrew Chapman was flat on the floor, completely limp like an animatronic with its battery ripped out.

His wife wailed and covered their son's eyes. He must've been eight years old. I felt real fuckin' bad for the kid. But before I had time to really reflect on all that, the bathroom door flung open and a man dove out toward the double-barrel shotgun on the floor.

I didn't know it at the time, but this man was Andrew's older brother, the addict they'd been supporting all these years, so naturally once he saw his little bro with a hole in the dome, something compelled him into action. He scrambled across the carpet and picked up the double-barreled shotgun. He looked at the thing like it was a strange contraption from a distant past or future. The man clearly had no firearms experience.

I pointed my pistol at him, and the woman on the couch shrieked. I pulled the trigger.

Now, I gotta tell you, in most circumstances, I can do basic math. But I was under a lot of stress right then. I guess it didn't occur to me that three plus three equaled six. Or rather, six minus six equaled me with a dumbass look on my face. I stared down the twin barrels of Andrew's shotgun, and then I turned around and ran out of there as fast as I could.

An explosion went off behind me, and I staggered to my knees. Hot pain needled through my left shoulder, and my arm went numb. The son of a bitch had managed to graze me. The brother came out of the motel with the shotgun in hand, raised it to his shoulder, and fired off another cannon blast in my direction.

That one missed me by a mile and a half, but goddamn did it fill my pants right up.

I got back into my car, switched the ignition, and high-tailed out of there. No doubt the police would show up any second. I drove down the road with my right hand. My other arm was completely numb. I could still pick it up and move it and use it, but I couldn't really feel much. That didn't seem good.

Shit, man. I'd seen so many movies by now, I knew it wouldn't matter. Not where I was going.

I PARKED DOWN THE STREET from Rachel's house and reloaded my gun with the extra bullets Joey had given me. Lucky for me, a revolver's a pretty simple piece of technology. You just stick the cartridges in the cylinder and pull the trigger. Just make sure you're on the right side of the barrel.

I gave Rachel one more chance. I called her twice, and she ignored both calls. So I took a deep breath and hid the gun in my pocket. I looked at myself in the mirror. My hair was mussed, and I was drenched in sweat. I combed my hair with my fingers and wiped my sleeve across my face. Nothing could make me look any less like a guy who was about to blow away his ex-girlfriend.

My shoulder was bleeding all over the place. It turned out I had only caught two pellets from the buckshot Andrew's brother sent my way. But that was just enough to tear up my muscles and nerves and put my arm out of commission. I grabbed the cheap first-aid kit from the glove box, which had nothing better to offer than large Band-Aids. Shit, it was better than nothing. I covered the holes in my shoulder and flexed my fingers. My nerves were sore, but I wasn't disabled yet.

I got out of the car and started walking down the street. As far as I knew, Rachel's parents kept her afloat in this apartment. She didn't have a job, and I just assumed that girlfriend of hers wasn't paying the bills. I didn't want her to be collateral damage, but if she got between me and Rachel, I'd gladly put her in the ground.

The apartment campus was a good bit nicer than mine, an open-air style place with well-groomed trees, pretty little gardens, and even some working fountains. The only fountain at my apartment complex didn't work, and it was all gross and mildewed over. I retraced my steps from when I left in shame the last time I was here.

When I found her door, I knocked loudly — like a cop or a land-lord — and pressed myself flat against the wall. She must not have seen me through the peephole, because she opened the door and stuck her head out to look around. That's when I sprang on her. I rushed her down and pulled the pistol from my pocket in one swift motion, and then I grabbed her by the sweater and pressed the gun against her collar.

"Hi, Rachel," I said. "Let's go inside."

Her face was frozen in shock. She opened her mouth like she wanted to say something, but no words came out. I dragged her inside and threw her on the floor, then I locked the door behind me and led her into the living room. Blood trickled in a light trail everywhere I walked. It occurred to me this might be inconvenient if one or two of these women ended up dead.

"Who was that?" said Rachel's partner from the kitchen. She was mixing drinks and slicing a lime at the counter, and she turned and looked at me with an expression like her worst nightmare had just come true.

I pointed the gun at her and said, "Put down the knife."

It clattered in the sink, and she backed against the fridge with her hands up.

"Get over here," I said. "Sit on the couch with your little girl-friend."

Rachel started sobbing and said, "Please."

"Please what?"

"Don't do this."

"I haven't done shit," I said. "We're just getting started."

They sat close together on the couch with their sweating hands clenched to the cushions and their bodies rigid with terror. I paced in front of them and savored the moment. Looking back, it was a bit much. I didn't need to make such a big and dramatic thing about it. I just needed to get the job done and get out of there.

I stopped in front of them with my elbow bent at my waist and my revolver leveled at the two women. It wasn't aimed at either of them, just sort of between them. They could've rushed me down and stopped me, but not without one of them getting shot. That was the whole point — put their lives in each other's hands so neither of them dared to make a move.

"I'll just bring up the ol' elephant in the room," I said. "I think you fucked me, Rachel."

She twisted her brows and said, "What?"

"Not literally. I mean, I guess literally, too. But this is my theory: you were fucking Gilbert. Again, literally. And you didn't mean to tell him. It just sorta came out. Kind of like an orgasm."

"What the fuck are you talking about?" she barked. "I've never had sex with Gil, you fucking asshole."

"Then how the fuck did his crew get onto me so quick?" I yelled back.

"I don't know," she said. "I never said shit. Who else knows about it?"

"Shut up. Doesn't matter. You're a loose end. I bet you fuckin' told *her* already." I gestured at her girlfriend. "Who the fuck even are you, anyways?"

"Lilith," she stammered.

"Fuckin' Lilith. What are you, some kind of biblical angel?"

She didn't have an answer to that question.

"Whatever," I said. "There's just one angle I didn't consider." I fixed the barrel back on Rachel. "We went to school together. You, me, Gil, Joey, and Andrew."

"I never talked to any of them except Gil," she said. "And we only ever talked about jobs. Working for his dad."

"Bullshit."

I kept moving the barrel left, right, left, right, fixing on each of their faces. Panic overwhelmed me. Every second that passed just pushed the tension closer to me pulling the trigger and getting it over with. But I needed information first.

"Give me your phone," I said.

Rachel obeyed. She took a smartphone off the coffee table and handed it to me.

"Toss it," I said.

She threw the phone, and it bounced off my stomach and hit the carpet in front of my feet. I resisted the urge to bend over and grab it like I normally would. Instead I kneeled carefully, keeping my eyes and the barrel of my gun fixed on them. I picked up the phone with my off hand, but the screen was locked.

"What's the passcode?"

"Five-eight-six-nine," Rachel said.

Right about then, it all tied back to me feeling like the world's biggest dumbass. All of this tracked. I checked her call log, her text messages, and... well, she was getting more dick than I expected, but I guess that was part of her and Lilith's arrangement. Unless she had deleted them all in advance, there was no communication with Andrew or Gil.

I tossed the phone back at her and said, "Maybe you deleted the evidence."

"Come on, man," Rachel pleaded. "I can't prove I didn't do something. You gotta believe me."

That's when the whole world's biggest dumbass thing merged into something new. Now I felt like the world's biggest asshole. Something in her voice told me she wasn't lying, or if she was, it was a really goddamn convincing lie. The gun shook in my hands.

She sniffled and said, "Please, Tristian."

I let out a breath. Then I pointed the barrel between Rachel's eyes, and I pulled the trigger. Her partner yelped.

The gun clicked on empty. Rachel opened her eyes, welling with tears, and I smiled at her.

"Maybe next time," I said.

I tried to make it kinda flirty, but I just sounded like a ghoul. I opened the cylinder of my revolver and took out the empty casing I'd left. There were five live rounds in case I needed them. But I had a feeling Rachel and Lilith weren't in much shape to do anything to me. And with enough luck, they wouldn't go telling anyone what I'd told Rachel.

I backed away from them slowly, and the gun twitched in my hand. I opened the door behind me and stared them down until I was out in the hallway, then I shut the door and ran the hell out of there.

I FEEL REALLY BAD ABOUT the whole thing in retrospect. It was too much. I was never gonna shoot her, but I thought I had to make a good act out of the whole thing. But in retrospect, knowing Rachel had nothing to do with anything except she fucked me once and I spilled my purse all over her lap — well, let's just say it was a lot for me to handle.

The liquor store was locked up and dark when I drove by. I went down the street and parked in the lot behind the coffee shop, which was pretty packed this time of night. No doubt the patrons were there for coffee and not anything that resembled illegal gambling. I left my car in the rear corner next to a rotten fence and a line of palm trees separating the lot from an abandoned auto shop.

The coffee shop was busy as hell, full of chatter and singing and arguments and freewheeling. Just walking by the place, you got the idea that they served more than coffee. I buried my hands in my pockets and walked down the street toward Calvin's Liquors. I cut through the alley halfway there and hopped a fence. Then I unlocked the back door and went inside.

There was nobody around, as far as I could tell. The parking lot was completely empty. I got the keys from my pocket and let myself in, then I locked the door behind me just to be sure. The door marked **PRIVATE** was open, and a light was on inside the office. I held my pistol forward with a shaking hand and went inside.

The office was empty. Whoever'd been here had left already. They had ransacked the place and left a bunch of garbage everywhere.

The first thing I noticed was a pair of first-class tickets to Key West. Poor Calvin, I thought. The last remnant of his last happy memory. I picked up the tickets and read them over.

But these tickets were one-way, and they were scheduled for yesterday. Now I hadn't slept much, and time was getting away from me a bit, but I knew that didn't add up. The names listed were Calvin Lenard and Vidya Iyer. And that was when it all came together.

The son of a bitch was leaving with his mistress. Now this part's speculation, since I have no proof one way or another, but there's really only one way I can think that would explain how he might fund such a venture.

He was gonna rip off the Viet mob. Just like me and Joey.

I crumpled the tickets and tossed them away. Goddamn, was I pissed off. I couldn't believe that bastard had fucked me like this. I had put my whole life on the line to try to keep him safe, but he had the same stupid fucking plan as Joey all along.

And the same stupid plan as me, I guess.

I checked the security tapes to see who might've been through the office and learned this info too. But everything from the last six hours had been erased. Somehow that made the whole thing clearer to me and that much more frightening.

Then I heard the lock click. I shut the light off and hid under Calvin's desk. I sat there as quietly as I could manage and listened for the intruders. Joey's voice was the first I heard, followed by Annie's. My heart was slamming against my ribs, and I tried my best to think up some excuse to give them, but nothing came to mind.

"Hey," came Joey's voice. "Did you turn off that light?"

"What light?" Annie said.

"In the office."

"No."

That's when the sounds stopped altogether, and I was fuckin' trembling with panic. It wasn't worth getting accidentally shot. I might as well try my luck, I figured. I stood up from behind the counter and announced myself.

"It's just me." I hid my gun in my pocket and raised my hands. "Don't shoot."

"Tris?" Joey said. He came inside and flicked on the office lights. Annie waited behind him, her eyes glancing between the front and back door like she thought I had backup coming in to blow them away.

"Yeah." I sounded sheepish, and I couldn't help it. "Sorry, man. I was gonna call you back."

"What the fuck, man? Why'd you plug Nico?"

"He was covering his own ass," Annie grunted.

"I had to go," I said. "Fuckin' emergency. Wasn't gonna just leave him there like that."

"So you just killed him," she said. "Like the cold-blooded killer you are, mister killer man?"

"I don't think so," Joey said. "This guy's no killer. But he fucked up, one way or another."

"What are you talking about?" I tried to force out a laugh, but it wasn't that convincing. "Fuckin' Shakespeare over here."

"I know it was you," he said in a low monotone. Annie stood behind him with a stony expression on her face. They were both giving me the death stare, ready to draw and shoot at any wrong move. This must've been my fiftieth *I'm fucked* moment in the last couple weeks.

"What was? What are you talking about?" I tried my best to look confused, but I was never that good a bullshitter.

"You thought you covered your ass," Annie barked. "But you were wrong."

"We found Andrew's family," Joey said. "His fuckin' brother's some piece of work, huh? Blasted a shotgun two feet away from my head. Almost fuckin' killed me. But I put a hole in his brain."

"What?" I said.

"Yeah," he continued. "His wife and son were fuckin' terrified. I guess some asshole came in in and blew away the man of the house. But lucky for us, he'd already been talking."

"He did, did he?"

"Yeah," Joey said. "I guess he had some partner named Tristian. Crazy thing, huh? What a weird coincidence."

"So what do you want," I said, "an apology?"

"I want your take. Andrew's, too."

"Andrew's half is gone. He spent it on a new car."

"Yeah, I saw that," he said. "We took the coupe, right after we took his wife and kid. So what about you? How much have you spent?"

"Son of a bitch," I said. "You killed them? Why?"

"I said, how much did you spend?"

"None of it. I've got it all on me, all forty-seven-point-five."

He raised his hand, and I flinched, expecting to get shot. Then I felt like a dipshit when the searing pain and instant death didn't come. He held out a palm for the money. Even Annie kept her weapon concealed, and her eyes were darting around like a cokehead watching out for helicopters.

I'm not the kind of guy who believes in fate, miracles, guardian angels, or any other spiritual bullshit. Even in spite of how this whole business turned out for me, I don't think anything's predetermined. I believe we can change our fate. But sometimes fate just grabs you by the balls or the titties or the what-have-you and takes you for a goddamn ride. That was one of those times. I thought I was dreaming when the doors burst open and I saw the flashlights and heard that fuckin' cop, Detective King, screaming orders at my good friends.

The next few moments went by in a blur. Joey panicked and didn't know what to do, but Annie seemed to have this contingency all worked out. She drew her pistol, ducked behind the register counter, and took a pot shot through the chip racks where the detective was hiding. The blast practically deafened me, and everything was ringing in my world when I made my break for it.

Joey was glancing around, all confused like, and thinking back, it might've been a good time to take my gun and put a bullet through his skull. I'd have been better for it, even if that meant going to prison. Instead, I shoved him aside and ran through the crossfire, ducking while Detective King returned fire at the register counter. I felt a bullet fly past my ear and stumbled face-flat on the ground. It was a proper shootout. Just a few feet away, Annie squeezed off shots while Detective King moved around to a new position.

I didn't want any part of this. I got to my feet with my shoes squeaking on the tile floor, and I got out of there as fast as I could. I booked it down the sidewalk, but I knew I wouldn't get far before

Joey caught up and capped me in the back. I thought about the coffee shop where I'd parked. I didn't want to get any random people involved, but maybe I could duck in the parking lot and hide behind some cars until King's backup got here.

I heard footsteps echoing in the street behind me, and I pumped my feet and swung myself into the alley behind the coffee shop. The parking lot was small, four rows of about six cars each. Fuck, was this a bad idea or what? For a second there I wished I'd stayed at the liquor store.

A loud crack sounded off behind me, and a bullet snapped next to my head on the concrete wall of the coffee shop. I ducked down and ran into the parking lot. There was a big light at the rear of the coffee shop, and I didn't see anyone outside. I ran past the light and ducked into the middle row of cars.

Joey walked out into the parking lot with his Kahr K9 pistol hovering ahead of him. He scanned the lot, breathing heavy and fast. I heard him before I saw him, but then I'd probably die before I saw him.

"You aren't hiding now, aren't you?" he said. My heart jumped, and it took all my restraint not to take off running. I'd been watching him through the windows of a Ford F-150, but then he turned in my direction and I ducked down. His footsteps were getting louder.

I took the revolver out of my pocket and checked the cylinder. Five bullets were loaded up minus the empty I'd used to scare the shit out of Rachel.

I clicked the gun shut as quietly as I could, then I crept behind the Ford pickup truck and ducked across the gap to the next aisle. I kneeled behind a black BMW and glanced around as best I could without giving myself away. My hand trembled, and I wondered if I could even make my finger squeeze a bullet at my own friend.

Joey swung around the Ford truck and pointed his pistol. For a second there, I thought he might fire off a stray round and prompt somebody inside to call the cops. But I wasn't that lucky.

"Where are you?" he called out. "Come on, you fuckin' pussy."

He walked out into the aisle with his head high and his pistol aimed forward. He didn't seem worried about getting ambushed.

Overconfidence was a bitch, and I was gonna demonstrate that fact. But then he looked right at the BMW where I was hiding, and I ducked down and scrambled away.

The night cracked with three shots. The first bullet rang off the metal of the BMW, and the second broke the windshield of the Porsche right next to it. Then the third bullet went right through my back and out my front, right underneath my ribcage.

I couldn't believe it. The pain was worse than I'd imagined. Like getting hit with a sledgehammer and stabbed with a hot needle at the same time. I groaned and crawled away from Joey.

"It's over, man," he said. "Don't make it harder on us."

I dragged myself down the aisle until I reached the last car, a dark green two-door Miata. What a shitty car to be stuck behind. He was following me and knew my exact movements. Hell, he could probably see the blood trail behind me. I gasped for air and tried to make a run for it, but my legs collapsed, and I hit the asphalt. A shock of pain seared up and down my spine. I took cover behind that piece of Japanese shit, aimed over the engine block, and took my shots at Joey.

The first one was the hardest to fire. I'd heard all kinds of horror stories about stray bullets in public. Babies killed by stray bullets. I knew those things could go anywhere. But once I fired the first time, it just felt natural to empty the rest of the cylinder. I stood up from the engine block, smoke pouring from the gun in my hand.

Joey got up from behind a gray Honda Civic. He approached me unharmed with his pistol fixed at my head. I kept squeezing the trigger, and the gun kept clicking. Warm liquid flowed down my stomach and soaked my crotch. I knew I didn't have much time left, but I didn't have a lot to say. I just looked at him with eyes that said *get it over with*.

"Why?"

"Why what?" I said.

"You were like my brother," he said. "I loved you."

"Could've fooled me. You were always a fuckin' asshole. Tried to put me between you and the Viet mob, and for what? Two thousand bucks on a ninety-five K take? And you thought it was two mil, you fuckin' scumbag."

For the first time, Joey looked genuinely hurt. His eyes were like a kid who'd just been told his best friend doesn't want to play anymore. I actually felt kind of bad for the guy. But then he raised the pistol and aimed the barrel between my eyes.

"Doesn't matter now," he said. "You put your life in the pot. And buddy, you just bust out."

The parking lot came alive with the bright flash of an explosion. For a second there, it was like daytime. Maybe time slowed down in my head, or maybe I was just losing too much blood, but I jerked and fell to the ground. My stomach pumped blood, and I was getting weak. But as far as I could tell, I had no fresh wounds. Did he miss me?

Then I saw Detective King's face hovering over mine, and I realized no, he didn't miss. He hadn't fired at all. Joey coughed and writhed on the ground across from me. He tried to say something, but no coherent words came out.

"Don't worry," King replied. "That's just beanbag shot. You'll be all right."

"What's going on?" I moaned.

King kneeled next to me. "You're all right. Ambulance is on the way."

"Is she okay?"

"Who?" King said.

"Rachel."

"I don't know who that is," she said. "Just hang tight. Everything's gonna be okay."

I knew right then, like I always know, that everything was not all right. Everything was the opposite of all right. Nothing in the history of anything had ever been all right. The detective pulled a trauma kit from her utility belt and patched up the goopy hole in my belly. A few minutes later, a trio of overweight detectives arrived at the scene and stood in key vantage points while they muttered and chuckled to each other. There I was, struggling to keep my hold on this precious life, and these assholes were standing around like uncles at a barbecue. It pissed me off so badly that I blacked out.

12

I WOKE UP IN THE HOSPITAL with the distinct feeling I was overstaying my welcome in this world. My feet were numb, and it took weeks until I could stand up straight without someone holding me up. The movies never really talk about how a bullet in just the wrong place can fuck you up good for life. In my case, Joey's shot grazed my spine and caused nerve damage and permanent paralysis in the two smallest toes of each foot. The doctors said if it had been a millimeter closer to the center, I'd be a paraplegic.

Physical therapy went on for months and, naturally, it wasn't cheap. We're talking tens of thousands of dollars here. Calvin's Liquors doesn't exactly have a robust medical plan, and I didn't have much in my savings in the first place. So, naturally, I'm pretty deep in the fuckin' red here.

As you might've guessed, there was no accounting for that envelope I had on my person when I passed out. You know the one I mean — I told them how important it was to me, and they just shrugged and gave me that dumb-ass frown. When I pressed the issue, they threated to charge me with this and that bullshit. So I got out of there before I got myself into any more trouble.

Nobody bothered to fill me in on the details, but I learned what happened from watching the news. Anh "Annie" Phan was killed in the firefight with Detective Erin King. Even though they arrested Joey Patrone for shooting me, they pretty much dropped that charge once his DNA was connected to that cooler which turned up with the remains of Calvin Lenard. As it turns out, the camera from the adjacent car lot caught a volatile argument between Calvin and Joey that same night. Shooting me just gave them cause to take his DNA without consent, and that was that.

Apparently, the FBI had been mounting a case against Dennis Phan for the last five years. They were worried he might get killed in the street now that Adrien, his main muscle, and Annie, his heir, were both dead. His organization had been gutted. The feds pulled the trigger on some weak-ass tax charges that would get him seven years at best before he's back on the street. Most likely sooner with good behavior and some cooperation.

Not that I gave a fuck about Dennis or the case against him. It was all bullshit to me. The cops wanted me to testify against him, but what the fuck could I say? I never met the man in my life. They asked me to testify to some shit that never happened, but I knew that was a one-way ticket to the torture chamber. No way was I gonna do that.

Detective King visited me in the hospital. She seemed friendly enough at first, but I knew what this was about. She asked me about the gun I had on me.

"According to the FBI report," she said, "that same gun was used in another murder."

"That was Joey's gun," I said. "I took it out of his car right before you found us in the parking lot."

"Is that right," King stated plainly.

"Would I lie to you?"

She gave me a funny look and didn't answer that question. Then she closed her notepad and left the hospital room.

Next time I heard about the gun, it turned out Joey had eaten all my charges. That shocked the hell out of me. He took the fall for murdering Andrew — I guess they had him for Calvin's murder, not to mention Andrew's wife, brother, and kid, so he might as well eat every last murder and let me off the hook. Never in my life did I consider Joey might do something like that for me. If I were a thinking man, I might feel bad, like I'd misjudged him. But I didn't let it bother me.

I stayed in the hospital another couple weeks after Detective King stopped by and told me I was in the clear. The bills were piling up, and I was already broke and in debt. I had no way of paying anything. So they just gave me a cane and kicked me out. Nowadays I use a nice walnut walking cane I bought off the Internet, but back then I used the rubber-and-plastic piece of shit they sent me off with. It killed me to walk more than twenty steps without a rest, but on the other hand, it got me a medical marijuana license, so now I have a legal excuse to chief up in public.

Dennis Phan pled guilty to his charges and got his sentence reduced to four years. In the meantime, his dumbass son Brandon steered the ship as best he could, filling the duties for an absent Dennis and Annie. His first order of business was to make me manager of Calvin's Liquors. At first it was a relief, knowing I wouldn't have to deal with some new asshole boss. But then I realized — *I'm* the new asshole boss.

The upside of getting shot is that now I've got the prime parking space at work. I have a disabled placard hanging in my window, so I can park in the blue spot right next to the door out front. It was easier getting in on this side, plus I felt a bit less exposed coming and going.

Unfortunately, it was all on me to get Calvin's Liquors up and running again. It turned out some crooked cop with the SJPD — whoever had been feeding tips to Annie — was responsible for smashing the place up. They falsely reported Gilbert's crew fleeing the scene, but nobody ever looked into the case, so even though Marty was dead and Nico was in a skag coma, and neither of them could possibly have committed the crime, all the cleanup and accounting for the damage fell on me. When I filed for the city to pay for the damages, the district attorney politely told me to go fuck myself.

It was all mind-boggling enough, but worse yet, I had to interview people to replace myself and Joey as the two dipshits who run the place. And you wouldn't believe the kind of people who apply to this kind of work.

One guy showed up half-dressed, holding a beer can because he thought the job was all about chilling out and exchanging money for booze. Once I started explaining his responsibilities vis-à-vis the backroom and stock, he dipped out. Right in the middle of the interview. I wanted to go out there and clock the guy for wasting my time.

I didn't really wanna deal with this bullshit, so I settled on the first two people I interviewed who didn't piss me off. This turned out to be a pair of women who were, like, friends or lesbos or something like that. One of them had that dye-tipped hair like Rachel's girlfriend, and they were always talking and laughing like me and Joey used to, so I got the impression something might be going on there.

I came in one Tuesday morning feeling like absolute dogshit after I drank too much and slept too little. Hailey Van de Laar stood out front with a cigarette. The sun shined on her black hair, which looked like it'd been dipped in a vat of conditioner and left to rest in flat bangs like an unkempt and overgrown take on the Mia Wallace bob. Her eyes sagged purple, and she wasn't wearing makeup, so she looked tired as hell.

Hailey gave me a nod and blew a puff from her cigarette.

I nodded back and said, "Sorry I'm late."

She shrugged and said nothing. It was only five minutes past eleven, and I hadn't expected them to be there already. I went inside, and Emma Len was manning the counter, her bleached blond hair long and mussed like Hailey's, only tied into a knot or a bun or some such, with hot pink tips.

"Hey, Tris," she said. I nodded back and smiled. They were nice gals, even if they were rowdy lesbians or whatever. I minded them less and less every day.

Like most days, I spent every minute I could muster hiding in my office. There were some emails to answer, papers to sign, the occasional supply chain issue to resolve. But I did as little actual work as possible, and after some time I began to suspect Calvin had done the same thing. I knew for a fact that Brandon never lifted a finger while he was here, but who could blame him? He only ran the place for a few days, and he clearly never gave a shit.

Emma knocked on my door and called out, "Hey, Tris? Someone's here to see you."

"Who is it?" I called back.

"It's Emma. You've got a visitor."

"No, goddamnit. I mean who's the visitor?"

"Oh, right. It's some guy called Gil Rodriguez. He says wants to see you."

I never got that revolver back after the cops seized it. But I did go out and buy myself a new piece — a Kahr K9, just like Joey used to carry. Don't ask me how I got it. Anyway, I racked the slide, held it behind me, and answered the office door. I peeked through the doorway and saw Gil's grinning face.

"Hey, man." He put his hands up, then raised his shirt and did a little twirl just to prove he wasn't armed. "Mind if I come in?"

"Gimme one sec." I shut the door and stuck my pistol into a holster fastened underneath the desk. Apparently Calvin had put it there, but his gun was long gone when the office became mine. I answered the door again and let Gil inside.

The beefy little guy came in and took the chair across from my desk. It felt good being the boss of this place. Yeah, it was a shitty little liquor store, but at least I was in charge of something. I crossed my legs and kept myself straight as possible. My arms were fixed on the rests of my chair, ready to grab the gun from under the table in case things went south.

"So look at you," Gil said with a grin. "Chief Bossman, master of rivers and all who hydrate."

I laughed and said, "Sure, whatever, man."

"I'm happy for you, man. Rachel always told me you never liked Calvin. Seems like it worked out for you."

I said nothing.

"Anyway," he continued. "Now that he's out of the picture, I've got an offer for you."

"No," I said.

He chuckled. "But I didn't even—"

"Whatever it is, I'm not interested. I'm already bending over backward to keep the books balanced here. Last thing I need is to take some more off the top and find a way to explain where all that went."

He pursed his lips and nodded like he was turning over a serious decision in his head. Then he folded his hands under his chin. "Okay," he said. "If that's what you want, I can be an asshole about it."

"About what?"

"My money. The twenty-five thousand dollars you and Joey stole."

I shrugged and said, "I don't have it."

He put up his palms and said, "Look, I know Joey's in prison. His half's long gone, so I'm gonna be cool about it. I just need your half — twelve-point-five."

I shrugged and said, "I'm telling you, man. I never saw a dime of that money. Joey kept it all for himself."

He grimaced and made a broad gesture with his hands like a godfather making an offer you can't refuse. "Are you sure?"

"What are you gonna do?" I growled. "Have your friends stick me up?"

Gil laughed and waved me off. "Of course not. I just wanted to give you a chance to make things right and get in on this new thing I'm doing."

"Well, whatever it is," I leaned back in my chair and folded my hands behind my head, "you can shove it up your ass."

He stood up and cleared his throat, then he nodded and left without saying. I just watched the son of a bitch go.

After he was gone, I slipped out back to smoke a cigarette. Hailey and Emma were sitting in those shitty plastic chairs behind the counter me and Joey used to hang around in. The evening was overcast, with gray rain clouds, and I let the door shut behind me and sparked up my smoke. Everything was finally starting to cool off and feel all frosty and wintery. I blew a puff of smoke and watched the sky.

I looked through the messages on my phone and found the last log with Rachel. I'd texted her a few times but never heard back since that night. Understandable, I guess. I wouldn't wanna talk to me either. I stuck the phone in my pocket and dragged on the cigarette as hard as

I could, until it burned my lungs, and I blew a huge white tobacco whiff. Still, I felt nothing.

I went inside, locked up the office, and took off for the day. Hailey and Emma paid me no mind. I figured I'd keep my mouth shut and act like I was just stepping out so they didn't just close up early and go home to smoke weed and bang or whatever it was they did in their free time. I headed home to my apartment.

When I got back, Marianne was standing in the kitchen frying eggs while her boyfriend chopped vegetables. I didn't know the guy's name, and I didn't care. But he took up Joey's recently vacated spot on our apartment lease, so he helped keep us afloat. So I guess he was fine in my book.

I went past the kitchen toward the room, and Marianne stopped me cold by saying my name. "Hey, Tristian."

It might've been the first time I'd ever heard her say it. The word struck me strange and foreign. For a while there, I wasn't sure she even knew my name. "Yeah?"

"Some cop came by and left her card. Said she needed to talk to you."

I swallowed all my nervous fear and said, "Let me guess. Erin King?"

"That's right."

I called the detective, and she told me she had my property and wanted to return it. Apparently there was some "mix-up" involving a crooked cop and the cash in my envelope. She waited for me at the coffee shop down the street from Calvin's Liquors. She said she'd be there for ten minutes. After that, she wasn't responsible for my property.

I raced over there as fast as I could. When I got inside, she was sitting at a booth facing the entrance. There was a manila envelope sitting on the empty opposite side of the table. By the look of it, it was the same envelope I'd lost the night I got shot.

It was painful getting up and sitting down, so I often didn't bother sitting down when I went to meet with people. But I figured courtesy might do me some favors here, so I sat down and set the walking cane against my seat.

The detective's appearance hadn't changed a bit since I first met her. She still had that military-style buzzed hair and plain blue jeans under a sweatshirt emblazoned with the badge of the SJPD.

"How are you holding up these days?" she said.

"Fantastic," I said. "What do you want?"

"There's no need to be rude. Order something. I'll cover the tab."

"I'm not hungry. I've got a business to run."

"Well, I won't hold you up. I just thought you might want this back." She shot her eyes down at the envelope, then back up at me. "I understand it was stolen off your person when you checked into the hospital."

"How much is in there?" I said.

"I didn't check," King said. She stood up from the booth and took out her wallet, then she dropped a twenty on the table. "Get something on me."

That was nice of her, I thought. A little too nice. I watched her walk out the coffee shop door, and that was the last time I saw her. I hope I never see her again. I opened the envelope and counted the money inside.

There was only nine hundred and fifty dollars.

I stared in that envelope with my mouth open and my eyes frozen. I couldn't believe it, but at the same time, it was what I'd seen coming all along. A waitress came over and asked if I wanted something, and in my blind fury I told her to fuck off. Then I stuck the twenty into the envelope and went home to get some sleep.

So here I am: nine hundred and seventy dollars to my name, and I owe seventy K to the mob. But I've got an idea. See, Brandon's got no clue what he's doing, so he's hiring muscle left and right. Guys he barely even vets except the obvious, like making sure they're not cops or whatever.

These days, Brandon runs those VIP games in the back of the coffee shop. I know when they go down and who's gonna be there. One of these days, when there's a bunch of high rollers throwing chips around, I'm gonna take my gun and kick in the door and hold them all up Billy the Kid style. I'll take everything they've got — their money, their valuables, and maybe even their lives.

I just need another hand for this job. A gun I can trust to watch my back when we're in a room full of bad guys who are itching to shoot somebody. And I figure you're the person I trust more than anybody right about now.

You wanna go all-in with me?

www.ingramcontent.com/pod-product-compliance
Lightning Source LLC
Chambersburg PA
CBHW050901180626
46814CB00007B/2824